United in Holy Deadlock

Nanci M. Pattenden

United in Holy Deadlock

Copyright © 2022 Nanci M. Pattenden

This is a work of fiction. All characters, names, incidents, organizations, and dialogue in this novel are either the products of the author's imagination or are used fictitiously.

Published by Murder Does Pay, Ink
Ontario, Canada
www.murderdoespayink.ca

ISBN: 978-1-7770778-8-4 (print)
e-ISBN: 978-1-7770778-9-1 (e-book)

1 2 3 4 5 6 7 8 9 0

Detective Hodgins
Victorian Murder Mysteries

Body in the Harbour

Death on Duchess Street

Corpses for Christmas

Books 1 to 3 Collection

Homicide on the Homestead

Generation Witch

Rebirth

D.E.M.ON. Tales Series

Assassin Eco-Corpses

Bobcat Got Your Tongue?

A Craptacular Understatement

Double Dog Dare Ya

Even Equines Don't Like Liver

ACKNOWLEDGMENTS

I'd like to say a great big thanks to Omar and Ashley, owners of Cardinal Press Espresso Bar in Newmarket for providing a wonderful environment in which to work. The coffee is constantly flowing and the treats are always yummy.

As always, thanks to my editor, MJ, of Infinite Pathways, and Chris, my graphics guru.

THANK YOU

CHAPTER ONE

When twelve-year-old Lizzie knocked on the freshly painted door of her neighbour's little clapboard house, the door swung open.

"Hello?"

No one answered.

"I've brought your wedding gown. Hello?" She pushed the door open far enough for her slight form to enter. "Mrs. Robinson? Mamma says Miss Olive needs to try the dress on one last time." She walked down the hall, calling as she went.

No one locked their doors, but it was strange to find it slightly ajar if no one was home. At almost 7:30 a.m., the kitchen showed no signs of breakfast being prepared.

Something should be cooking. Uncomfortable nosing around a neighbour's home uninvited, Lizzie hurried back down the hallway, out the front door, and swiftly home. *Mamma will know what to do.*

***

Lizzie held the wedding gown close to her chest as she hurried up the porch stairs, careful not to let it drag. She heard her mother in the kitchen washing the breakfast dishes. "Mamma!"

Mrs. Hogaboom turned. "What are you doing back so soon, and with the dress? You're old enough to do as you're told. Get back there right now."

"But Mamma…

"Don't interrupt me, girl. Go on, scoot before I tan your hide. There's only a few days left before the wedding."

Afraid to interrupt the scolding for bring the dress back, she waited until her mother paused. "Mamma, wait. Something's wrong. The front door was open. I called out, but no one answered." She reached for her mother's hand. "Come with me, please."

Mrs. Hogaboom grew concerned. "Wherever can they be? Olive is getting wed in two days. The house should be in a flurry of activity. Put the dress in the sewing room and we'll both go look." Mrs. Hogaboom grabbed her coat and hurried out the door.

Ten minutes later, Lizzie and her mother stood in the Robinson's kitchen. Mrs. Hogaboom walked to the wood stove and held a hand over it.

"Why, it's stone cold." She opened the little door in the front and peered inside. "No ashes, just fresh wood. Looks like someone cleaned it out last evening and readied it for the morning meal." She turned to Lizzie. "You check upstairs and I'll see if Mr. Robinson is in his workshop out back."

While her mother took one last glance around the kitchen, Lizzie tip-toed up to the second floor and peeked into the first room. *Empty.* She crept down the hall, jumping when a floor-board creaked under her foot. *Something's not right.* Lizzie opened the next door a few inches. A strange odour assaulted her nostrils. *What is that?* She opened the door further and screamed.

Mrs. Hogaboom reached for the handle on the workroom door when she heard Lizzie. She raced back into the house and up the staircase. Lizzie stood in the doorway of a bedroom, still screaming.

"Mamma!" Lizzie pointed.

The battered body of Olive lay sprawled across the bed, blood seeping through the white sheets.

Mrs. Hogaboom embraced her daughter. Lizzie buried her face in her mother's apron.

"Dear Lord in Heaven." Lizzie's mother pulled her away from the horrifying sight, downstairs, and out the front door. They ran across Wilton Crescent, hand-in-hand, and around the corner to their home at fifteen Pembroke Street. Fortunately, Lizzie's father had a rare day off due to repairs at the factory where he worked. He'd taken advantage of the time to do much needed repairs around the house.

"Elijah! Fetch the police. Something terrible has happened at the Robinson's." Between sobs his wife told him what she could, Lizzie still clutching her mother's arm.

***

Elijah Hogaboom ran the short distance to Station House Four, coat flapping around him, oblivious to the cold. Not used to running, he gulped in air as he tried to speak to the desk sergeant.

"There's been a murder. Someone come quick."

Barnes overheard and went over to the man, guiding him back to his desk. "I'm Constable Barnes. Take a deep breath and tell me what happened."

"My wife just came home and told me one of our neighbours is dead. Murdered. Oh, God. I just realized. There are three small children in the house." He stood and started pacing.

Barnes turned to the next desk and motioned for Riddell to fetch a cup of tea for Hogaboom.

"Please, sir. Sit and tell me exactly what happened. Take your time."

Hogaboom nodded at Riddell and accepted the tea. His hands shook, spilling the contents. He took a sip before starting.

"My daughter went to the neighbours with the wedding dress. Found her dead."

Barnes tried to fill out as much of the report as he could. Hogaboom stopped several times as he relayed the information from his wife. "Have the children been harmed?"

Hogaboom leaned forward, hands on Barnes' desk. "You've got to get someone out there right away. Check on the boys. My wife only mentioned Olive, but they never checked the rest of the house." He stood and started pacing again. "Said no one else appeared to be about. Grace's only thought was to get her out of there. She's hysterical."

"Your wife?"

"My daughter. She's the one who found her. She's hysterical."

Barnes stood and told Hogaboom to show him where the body was. Hogaboom wrung his hands as Barnes stopped at Riddell's desk to tell him to fetch the coroner.

"Tell him to come to…" Barnes turned to Hogaboom.

"Number four Wilton Crescent," Elijah said.

"And leave word for Detective Hodgins. He should be in any time." The constable hurried to catch up to Hogaboom, already heading out the door.

***

The pair hustled west across Wilton, dodging buggies on the way across Sherbourne Street, then around the bend. Barnes went into the Robinson residence first.

Hogaboom pointed up the stairs. "Wife said she's in the second room from the top of the stairs." He scurried out to the front porch to wait.

Barnes took a deep breath and headed up, checking the first room, just in case. The door sat half-open. Nothing seemed amiss. He pushed the door so hard it hit the wall. He let out a sigh of relief. *No one hiding.* Only an unmade bed, nothing out of place. He continued down the hall to the second room.

A young woman wearing her night clothes, stretched across a blood-cover bed. Barnes swallowed the bile building in the back of his throat. Backing out the door, he ran to the end of the hall and threw open the window, gulping in cold, fresh air. His throat burned, trying to keep the bile down. He stepped into the room across the hall from Olive's and spotted three beds, each containing a covered lump the size of a young child. Barnes pressed his hand to his chest, feeling the impression of the small silver cross his mother gave him when he graduated from Jarvis Collegiate.

"Please, not the children."

The room appeared untouched. No blood on the sheets. Barnes stood in the doorway, afraid of what he might find. There appeared to be no movement from any of the occupants. *Odd that they're still in bed.* He walked to the closest one and pulled back the crisp white sheet. The youngest boy opened his eyes. Barnes jumped.

"Who are you? Where's Mama?" The boy pulled the blanket back over his head and wailed. As the child's voice rose, the other two woke.

"You're a policeman." The oldest boy sat up. "Why is there a policeman in my house?"

"What's your name, lad?" Barnes moved to the next bed.

"Barney." He pointed to his brothers. "That one's Bart. The baby is Benny."

"I nots a baby." Benny lowered the blanket and sat up, arms crossed, pouting.

Barnes grinned. "No, you're a big boy. I need you to get dressed and come straight downstairs. Do you need help?"

All three shook their heads.

"Why are you still in bed? Young lads like you should be outside playing."

Barney swung his legs over the side of the bed. "We had a party last night for Olive. That's my sister. She's getting wed. Mamma let us stay up way past bedtime."

"That must have been fun. Now, hurry and dress."

Barnes crossed the hall and closed the door to Olive's room so the children couldn't see what happened to their sister. After hurrying them along, Barnes hustled the boys out to the front porch and over to their neighbour.

Barnes spotted the coroner's wagon and waved. Dr. Stonehouse maneuvered the rig down the street, Riddell holding on for dear life. Riddell jumped off before Stonehouse brought the horse to a stop.

"You don't look so good, Henry." Riddell slapped him on the back. "Maybe you should stay outside."

"It's not funny, Tom." He lowered his voice. "Their sister has been bashed about. So much blood. When I saw the children in their beds, I thought they'd been killed too." Barnes turned to Hogaboom. "Do you have any idea where their parents might be?"

Hogaboom shook his head, then dropped to his knees on the front lawn and embraced the boys. He looked at the constable. "What do I tell them?"

"Nothing yet. We'll wait until we know more." Barnes turned to Dr. Stonehouse. "Upstairs. The girl, Olive, is in the second room. I've yet to check the rest of the house."

Dr. Stonehouse set his bag down. He took out a small container of white powder and handed it to Hogaboom. "Give this to your daughter. It will calm her and allow her to sleep. Only a quarter teaspoon. If your wife needs it, she can have a full teaspoon. Mix it in a glass of water. From the looks of you, you could probably use it, too."

Hogaboom released the boys from his embrace and stood, taking the small glass jar from the doctor. "Thank you."

Barnes opened his notebook. "You'll have to stay a while longer and I'll need your address. The detective will have questions for your wife and daughter."

"Fifteen Pembroke. Just around the corner." He sat back down on the snow-covered lawn, leaning against a maple tree, staring at the small bottle of powder. The boys huddled close, still unaware of what had happened.

Riddell placed a hand on Barnes' shoulder. "Sorry. Can only imagine what went through your mind when you saw those boys. We'd better have a look around and see if we can find the parents."

"Robinson's a carpenter. Had a workshop out back," Hogaboom mumbled.

"I'll check there," Barnes said. Riddell gave him a nod and headed inside after him, branching into the living room while Barnes went through the kitchen and out into the backyard.

Robinson's workshop sat at the back of the property. As Barnes approached, he noticed the shop was silent. *There should be sounds of hammering, tapping of carving tools, or planing of wood. Nothing.*

He lifted the latch and opened the door a few inches. Silence. He opened the door farther to allow more sunlight in. The room contained tools of the woodworking trade, most hanging neatly on the wall. Nothing seemed amiss. Barnes stepped in and opened the small window. The early morning sun glinted off something on the worktable.

He walked over and picked up a chisel, noticing a blank nail on the wall where it would've hung from the thin leather strap on the handle. Several types of axes and hatches sat on the floor, propped against the wall. As he turned to leave, a pile of sacks caught his eye. Something dark puddled around them.

Barnes closed his eyes and said a silent prayer before going over. One by one, he lifted the sacks, stopping only when an arm appeared. He dropped the sack he was holding and ran back to the house. Riddell sat on the bottom step to the upstairs, cradling his head.

"I found Robinson."

Riddell looked up. "Dead?"

Barnes nodded.

"Found one woman in the sewing room. Another in the parlour. Not sure who they are. Probably the mother, and maybe a family member helping prepare for the wedding.

Still breathing, barely. Stonehouse treated them as best he could, and he's taken them to the hospital. Looks like they were hit with something blunt."

Barnes blanched as Riddell spoke, remembering the sight in Olive's room.

Hogaboom stood at the doorway, listening. "What about the baby?"

The constables exchanged a look, each one shrugging. Barnes answered. "We found no baby." He joined Riddell on the porch steps.

"Grandmamma has Susie. Is breakfast ready?" Barney stood with his arms around his brother's shoulders.

Hogaboom turned to Barnes. "Shall I take them to my house, or do they need to go to the police station?"

Benny wailed again. "Don't wants to go to jail!"

Riddell knelt in front of Benny. "Hush. No one's taking you to jail."

"Where's Mama?"

"She's gone to the hospital and asked Mr. Hogaboom to look after you. Would you like that?"

Benny sniffled, wiping his hand under his nose. He shrugged.

Hogaboom joined Riddell. "My Grace makes the best flapjacks. Would you like to try them?"

Benny nodded and looked at his oldest brother.

"How about it, Barnabas? You can stay for a few days, play with my young-uns."

Barnes raised an eyebrow. "Barnabas?"

"Yes. Barnabas, Bartholomew, and Bennett." Hogaboom pointed to each one as he said their name.

Barnes looked at the boys. "But you prefer Barney, Bart, and Benny?"

All three nodded.

"Why is Mama in the hospital?" Benny's eyes watered when he looked at Barnes.

"She's had a little accident. Go with Mr. Hogaboom. If you're good, maybe I'll give you a tour of the police station later."

Three heads nodded. Hogaboom took the boys over to his house, leaving Barnes and Riddell to wait for the return of Stonehouse and the arrival of Detective Hodgins.

"There'll be people coming to help with arrangements and such." Riddell waved towards the neighbour's house. "At least according to Hogaboom. We'll need to keep everyone out."

Barnes sighed. "Don't want to be the one to tell the young lady's fiancé. Better coming from someone he knows. Give him time to come to terms with it before the police talk to him. Maybe Mr. Hogaboom could do it?"

CHAPTER TWO

A half hour later, Hodgins arrived. *A murder so close to the station.* He looked at Barnes. *Can't be too bad. Henry isn't green.* "I understand we have a young woman who's been murdered."

Barnes stopped him before he entered the house. "Two people, actually. Two more injured. Thought there was a missing baby, but she's fine."

"What kind of deranged person would do such a thing?" Hodgins shook his head in disbelief. "Who reported it?"

"Mr. Hogaboom." Barnes pointed at the man walking towards them. "Actually, it was his wife and daughter who found them. He's taken the three boys who live here home to his wife."

"Mr. Hogaboom?" Hodgins, a tall, well dressed, distinguished-looking man, walked over to the man. "I'll need to speak with you. Could you come into the house?"

Hogaboom stood and slowly followed the detective inside.

"Barnes, which way to the parlour? May as well be comfortable."

"Wouldn't advise that, sir." Barnes waved to the right. "Kitchen would be better."

Hodgins nodded, understanding Barnes' meaning. "I see. Kitchen it is. Riddell, lock the front door and meet us inside. Don't want people wandering in. Barnes, take notes."

Once they were all settled, Hodgins asked Hogaboom to tell him what happened.

"Well, I suppose it started when Lizzie came over with the wedding dress."

Barnes looked up from his notebook. "Lizzie?"

"My eldest daughter. She's twelve. My wife is a seamstress and made Olive's wedding dress. Mrs. Robinson wasn't the best with a needle and thread. Wanted the dress to look perfect. Lizzie was bringing it over so Olive could try it on."

Barnes wrote hastily, trying to keep up. "Now, who's Olive? You mentioned her at the station."

"Olive Robinson. The young woman…" Hogaboom hesitated, still upset about the murder.

Barnes visualized the sight, then shook it off.

Hogaboom composed himself and continued. "Supposed to be getting married in a few days. Lizzie's the one who found her."

"Got a daughter not much younger," Hodgins said. "Wouldn't want her finding a dead body." *Cordelia would have my hide, but Sara's like me. She'd be more curious.* "What happened after she found Olive?"

"First trip over was with the dress. She thought the house was empty. Ran home to her mother. They both came back to check it out. My wife thought maybe Lizzie exaggerated. You know how children's minds work. Lizzie went upstairs and screamed. When my wife saw what caused the screaming, they both raced home. My wife sent me to fetch you."

The back door squeaked when Dr. Stonehouse came into the kitchen and nodded at Hodgins. "Front door's locked. Got the women admitted at Toronto General. Haven't seen anything this brutal for quite some time. Can't say for certain, not until I've done a complete examination, but they've probably been unconscious for several hours. It's a wonder those women survived as long as they have. Nasty wounds. The attack probably occurred last night, but I can't be sure.

"Did either woman say anything?" Hodgins asked.

"No. Both are still unconscious."

"Right." He turned to the constables. "Where were the two ladies found?"

Riddell cleared his throat. "Found the two women in the parlour. One is probably Mrs. Robinson, but we don't know who the other one is. Jacob Robinson is in his workshop, out back."

"What about the baby?" Hodgins asked. "You mentioned a baby. And who could the other woman be?"

"Baby's with the grandmother, but we don't know who the other woman is. My guess is a relative." Riddell pulled out a chair and sat at the table.

"Two dead, two injured," Hodgins said. "Why would anyone do such a thing?"

"I can't imagine." Hogaboom said. "Mr. Robinson was a carpenter, and well liked. Mrs. Robinson was very active with the church and headed several activities. I don't know of anyone who had a bad word to say against any of them. Even the children are extremely well behaved. For boys, that is."

"Thank you, Mr. Hogaboom. You can go home now." Hodgins noticed the man appeared agitated or nervous, looking through the window at the workshop, and back again. He'd been drumming his fingers on the table the entire time, one leg bouncing up and down like a nervous cat. "You tend to your family. I'll be by tomorrow to speak with them."

Hogaboom nodded and scampered back home.

Barnes tapped his notebook. "I have his address."

"Very good. I'd better have a look around." Hodgins stood and addressed the doctor. "Riddell can help load the bodies onto your wagon."

Hodgins turned to the constables. "Barnes, you check upstairs, Riddell, the parlour when you've finished with the doctor. Try not to disturb anything. Write down whatever looks amiss, out of place. You know what to do. I'll go to the workshop."

Riddell followed Stonehouse upstairs, Barnes close behind. Hodgins went looking for the workshop. *Poor Henry. He must have almost had a fit when he entered the boy's room. They're going to need a lot of love to get over what's happened.* Riddell spotted a small wooden structure in the corner of the property and went in. The body lay just as described, under the sacks, with one arm exposed. The canvas sacks had absorbed most of the blood, leaving little mess around the body.

He piled the sacks as he removed them. Robinson's head had been hit repeatedly with something hard, his overalls and smock soaked in partially dried blood.

The workshop was too dark to see much else. Hodgins picked up a lantern from a nearby shelf, lit it, then walked around the shop. Three carved table legs sat on the workbench, the fourth lay near the body splattered in blood. The walls also had blood on them, along with something else. He moved closer and held up the lantern. He recognized the foreign matter. *Brains.* Hodgins' stomach turned.

Stonehouse and Riddell came in and collected the body. They were careful to avoid touching anything, especially the small pool of blood.

With the corpse out of the way, Hodgins spent twenty more minutes searching the shop. He found a few smeared fingermarks on the inside of the door, and a broken fire poker. It was going to be difficult to determine who was attacked first.

Hodgins found a clean corner on the workshop bench and used that to sit and make notes in his book before returning to the house, careful to ensure he securely latched the workshop's door. The wildlife was stirring, and he didn't want a stray dog, squirrels, or whatever else prowled around early morning, drawn in by the blood and brain matter.

Hodgins entered the house through the kitchen door and found Riddell making tea. Barnes sat with his head cradled in his arms on the table top.

"Excuse the liberty, sir, but I just had to wash the taste of the blood out of my mouth. Odd how it seems to fill the air."

Hodgins grabbed a tea cup. "I understand completely. Good thing it's late fall. With the bodies lying around, well, you can imagine if it was mid-summer."

Barnes bolted for the door.

"Make his tea extra strong," Hodgins said. "Did you find anything?"

"Looks like they were done-in the same way. Heads bashed. All in their nightclothes except for Mr. Robinson. Hard to tell if they were retiring for the night, or just waking up."

Barely glancing up when Barnes returned, Hodgins made a note. "Did either of you find a murder weapon? There's a broken table leg in the workshop with blood on it, but it couldn't have inflicted all that damage. Too small."

Both constables shook their head.

The water finally boiled. Barnes poured it into the teapot where Riddell had placed the infuser of loose tea. Barnes brought the teapot to the table and let it steep. "Funny thing, sir. One of the ladies appears to have put a dress on over her nightclothes."

"Hmm, may mean the noise roused her from her sleep. Could her husband have been working late into the night? There were several lanterns, wicks burned down."

They compared notes and sipped tea in silence. Riddell gathered the cups once empty. "Too bad the tea leaves couldn't tell us the name of the killer." He was just finishing washing the cups when the front door creaked open.

Riddell forgot to re-lock it after assisting the doctor. A nosy neighbour wandered in. Barnes escorted him outside and noticed a crowd had gathered. The constables took advantage and started interviewing the neighbours.

Barnes spoke to the lady in the adjacent house.

"Saw them bodies being loaded inta the wagon. Have them what lived there been murdered?"

"It appears so. You live next door? Can I have your name?" Barnes asked.

"Etta Jones. Who'd wanna kill such nice folk?"

"That's what we're here to determine. Do you know of any relatives staying with them?"

"Flora's sister. Came in yesterday ta help with the wedding."

Barnes looked up. "Flora, ma'am?"

"Mrs. Robinson. Are they all dead? Poor Sam. That's Olive's young man. Weddin' was supposed to be Monday." She stopped suddenly and clasped Barnes' arm. "Susie!"

"Pardon?"

"The wee babe. Was she…?"

Barnes patted her hand. "The boys are fine, and the baby is with her grandmother."

Etta Jones sobbed. "The baby. Oh, my. All those poor children."

One of the other neighbours came over and guided Etta home. Most of the neighbours were in shock and couldn't provide much information. No one saw or heard anything.

Hodgins joined the constables on the front lawn. "Either of you know who was on this beat last night? Maybe he saw something."

Riddell spoke up. "Harrington. He traded shifts so one of the other lads could spend the evening with his parents for their anniversary."

"I found out a few things," Barnes said. "Mrs. Robinson's sister came in yesterday, so that might be the other woman in the parlour. The fiancé is Sam. The lady who told me got hysterical, and I didn't get his last name."

"Not to worry," Hodgins said. "One of Olive's friends lives across the road and came over to find out what happened. Fiancé's name is Samuel Wright. Got his address. I'll have a word with him later." *Not looking forward to that conversation.* "I've got the house key." He handed it to Barnes. "I want you two to go through every scrap of paper in the house. Look for anything that might help. Lock up when you're done, so no one enters while we're still investigating. Guess this will be in the late edition paper and everyone will know what's happened."

Barnes turned to Riddell. "I've had quite enough of the upstairs. Why don't you look around there and I'll go through the main floor and workshop?"

***

Barnes entered the sewing room where Riddell had found one of the unconscious women. A treadle sewing machine, the Singer name barely legible from age, sat by a window. The room didn't appear to get much use, as he couldn't see any fabric in the room, and the machine had a thin layer of dust on it.

Finding nothing, Barnes moved to the parlour where the other woman had been assaulted. The fireplace sat cold, a pile of unburned logs waiting for the strike of a match.

Most of the furniture hadn't been disturbed. One chair lay overturned beside the blood stains on the carpet. Besides chairs, a small table, and a chaise-lounge, the only other furniture was an embroidery frame with a half-finished design. Barnes went over to admire the peacock being stitched and noticed one tiny spot of blood on the white fabric. *Shame to have such a beautiful piece ruined.*

He turned to the game table. Something caught his eye, so he walked over. A single playing card lay on the carpet against the wall. He picked it up in case it was important, then opened the drawer. Just checker and chess pieces. Examination complete, he moved on to the main sitting room.

He found a small writing desk in the front corner, near the bay window, and started rifling through the papers; mostly correspondence with the relatives about the wedding. He smiled, thinking of his own recent nuptials. *If anything had happened to Violet…* he shook away the thought. One pile was returned wedding invitations. Another pile contained invoices for flowers, and fabric for the wedding dress. Each pile was neatly organized.

Nothing seemed peculiar, so Barnes started with the drawers. The first contained writing paper and a few postage stamps. The second, orders and invoices for Mr. Robinson's carpentry business. The third was locked. Barnes checked the little cubbyholes for the key. It was nowhere to be found. Not wanting to damage the desk, he made a note in his book. Maybe Hodgins had a way to open the lock without harming the beautifully crafted desk.

Barnes did a thorough search, but found nothing that could indicate a reason for murder. *Why would anyone harm such a seemingly nice family? If someone had a grudge against one of the family members, why not just kill that one person?* Barnes was about to head into the kitchen when someone rapped on the front door. Barnes hurried over.

A woman in her sixties stood on the front step, cradling a sleeping baby. She stepped back when Barnes opened the door, checking the house number.

She took in his uniform. "This is my daughter's home. Why are you here?" She pushed past him into the house.

"Forgot Susie's favourite doll. Flora? Where are you? Catherine?"

Barnes groaned, not wanting to be the one to tell her that her granddaughter had been killed and her daughters severely injured. "Please, ma'am, would you accompany me to the kitchen? I'm Constable Barnes. Who might you be?"

"Mrs. Shore." The woman looked confused. *Why are there police in my daughter's home?*

"I'm sorry, but there's been… an accident."

She sat at the table, rocking the baby. "What do you mean, accident? Where are my daughters?"

Barnes took a deep breath. "They've been injured, and your granddaughter and son-in-law are deceased."

It didn't sink in right away. "What do you mean? Stop talking nonsense. I spoke with Flora just last night. Where are the children?" She stood up. "Olive, darling, Grandmother's here."

Barnes guided her back into the chair. "Both your daughters are at Toronto General Hospital. The boys are with neighbours. The Hogabooms."

She clutched the baby to her bosom. "No." Her face scrunched and she shook her head in disbelief, sobbing louder than the neighbour had, waking the baby. "I want to see my daughters."

Riddell came downstairs to see who was causing such a ruckus. Together, they tried to console Mrs. Shore. Riddell took the baby outside to quiet her. Once away from her shrieking grandmother, she fell back asleep. He stood just outside the back door so Mrs. Shore could see the baby. Eventually her sobs softened, and she gestured towards Riddell to take the baby back.

"Mrs. Shore, can you think of anyone who might wish to harm the family? Even something that seems minor?" Barnes asked.

She rocked back and forth in the chair, holding Susie tight. "No. No one."

"A jealous suitor, maybe? Someone unhappy with Olive's upcoming nuptials?"

Mrs. Shore stopped rocking. She opened her mouth to say something, then changed her mind.

CHAPTER THREE

Hodgins stood with Sam Wright, the fiancé of the deceased bride-to-be, on his porch. He arrived just as Sam headed out the door and broke the bad news.

"You must be mistaken. I'm to be wed in a few days. Nothing's happened to Olive. She lives at number four Wilton. You must have gotten the address wrong. If you'll excuse me, I must get to class."

"Yes, number four. There's no mistake." Hodgins placed a hand on Sam's shoulder. "I'm sorry, but I need to ask you a few questions. Did you see your fiancé last evening?"

Sam dropped onto one of the wicker chairs, his head hanging down, too distraught to acknowledge the detective's questions. The sun shone brightly, contrasting the dismal atmosphere.

Hodgins reached over and touched the young man's shoulder. "Mr. Wright?"

Sam looked up. "Excuse me?"

"Last evening. Where were you? Did you see Miss Robinson?"

"No. We had lunch in the park, then I escorted her home. I haven't seen her since."

Hodgins wrote in his notebook. "Where were you last evening?"

"Out with my friends from school—University College. Studying mathematics, the arts, and French. Final year. I hope to be a teacher after I graduate. Got home rather late."

"I'll need the names of your friends."

Sam's eyes widened. "Are you suggesting I had something to do with Olivia's death? I'd never... I loved her."

"No, not at all. I just need to know where everyone was at the time of the attack. Process of elimination."

Sam studied Hodgins' face, then leaned back. "I understand."

He gave the detective the names of five people. "They'll vouch for me." A hint of a smile touched his lips. "At least those sober enough to remember."

The smile faded almost immediately. "Who would do such a thing? They had no enemies. Why would anyone harm them?"

Hodgins closed his notebook. "I don't know, son. But I plan on finding out. At least the baby and boys were spared any injury. It's a small consolation, though." He rose. "I'll contact you if I require anything further."

Hodgins walked back to Station House Four, a lot slower than usual. He'd never investigated an incident with so many victims at one time.

The wind picked up, blowing snow down his neck. He shivered, raised his collar, then fastened the top button on his overcoat. As he climbed the stairs to the station, he heard his name from up the street.

He stopped and turned. "Barnes. Is the house secure?"

"Yes, sir. Locked up tight. Riddell is escorting Mrs. Robinson's mother home. She gathered a considerable number of things for the baby. She's a widow and can't handle all the children on her own, so she'd agreed the boys will stay with the Hogabooms for now."

"Join me in my office." Hodgins entered the building, Barnes close behind.

Hodgins settled behind his desk. "Were you able to find anything of interest?"

Barnes sat opposite. "No. Well, maybe. One drawer in his desk is locked and I couldn't find the key. All sorts of correspondence piled on top of the desk. One drawer contained invoices and other financial papers." Barnes tapped his fingers on the arm of the chair. "If he didn't think it necessary to lock up private financial papers, what would he have that was so secret it had to be locked up?"

Hodgins leaned back. His chair shifted onto two legs. "That's an excellent question. I know I lock up financial papers. Only Cordelia knows where I keep the key. Jewellery would be in the bedroom. Anything overly expensive, I'd probably have the bank lock it up in their safe."

Hodgins righted the chair and opened his notebook. "I have the names of the people Sam Wright was with last evening." He checked his pocket watch. "It's still early. May as well confirm their whereabouts. They should all be at the university."

Barnes copied the names into his book, then they headed outside to catch the streetcar downtown. The university sat a few blocks from the stop.

Hodgins paused in front of one building and looked around. "I believe administration is in that one." He pointed north and they followed a path across the property. A sign in front confirmed they were at the correct location. Hodgins approached the secretary.

"Excuse me." He showed his badge. "We're looking for some of your students." He opened his notebook. "Lockerby, Adams, Gerrard, Simmons, and Thomms."

She looked from Hodgins to Barnes, then nodded and walked to a file cabinet. It didn't take long to find the files for the five students.

"Their schedules will be in the files." One by one, she opened the folders. Barnes wrote down the times, buildings, and the classrooms for the afternoon.

"Thank you, ma'am." Hodgins tipped his hat, and they went looking for the students.

"At least we won't have too far to go." Barnes tapped his book. "Three of them are in the same class."

"May as well speak to them together. Save a bit of time."

They found the first room in the adjacent building and Hodgins knocked on the classroom door. A tall and rather perturbed middle-aged gentleman opened it.

"I'm in the middle of a lecture. What do you want?"

"Detective Hodgins, Toronto Constabulary." He showed his badge. "I believe Messrs. Adams, Simmons, and Gerrard are in this class. Can you ask them to step out for a few minutes?"

The professor huffed, turned, then called the three young men. He shut the door as soon as they entered the hallway.

Adams looked at the constable, surprised to see a policeman waiting. "Is something wrong?"

Hodgins showed his badge again. "There's been an incident. I understand you were out last evening with Sam Wright?"

They all nodded. "Has something happened to Sam? We haven't seen him today."

"I'm afraid someone murdered his fiancé last night. Do any of you know Miss Robinson?"

"Murdered? How ghastly. Why would anyone want to kill Livy?"

Barnes had his pencil ready. "And you are?"

"Simmons." He gestured to the other two. "This one's Adams, and that's Stubby."

Barnes glanced at the tall, skinny student and grinned. "Stubby Gerrard?"

Hodgins broke in. "Mr. Simmons, you called her Livy. Did you know her well?"

"We've all been friends since we were children. She always tagged behind Sammy, so we weren't surprised when they started courting. Never imagined she'd grow up so nicely." He waved his hands, forming an hourglass shape. "Skinniest child I ever saw. Even Stubby wasn't that thin."

Simmons placed a hand on his friend's shoulders. "We should pay our respects. Sam must be devastated. Her family, too."

Hodgins and Barnes exchanged a look.

"What it is, Detective?" Adams asked.

"It'll be in the papers soon enough. They also killed her father. And her mother and aunt have been severely injured."

None of them spoke.

"You didn't answer my question. Were you with Mr. Wright last evening?"

"Yes. We were celebrating his upcoming wedding." Adams stared at Hodgins. "Wait. You aren't thinking Sammy did it?"

"Just confirming his whereabouts. Where exactly where were you celebrating?"

"At my home," Simmons answered. "Playing cards and drinking."

Adams and Gerrard agreed.

"Thank you."

Barnes checked the room number for the other two students. They confirmed the information the other lads provided.

CHAPTER FOUR

Before heading home for the day, Hodgins detoured to the coroner's office for a preliminary report.

Stonehouse smiled when the detective opened the door. "I believe I can guess why you're here."

"I wish I could say it was a social visit, but unfortunately, that's not the case. Have you been able to find anything I can use?"

"If you mean can I tell you what the murder weapon is, the answer is no. It appears the wounds are from different things. The table leg you found in the workshop matches the shape of some of the wounds on Mr. Robinson. Something else was used to bludgeon Olive, and she was stabbed as well. I believe Mr. Robinson was killed first, and the table leg simply dropped.

"It will be several days before I can give you a complete report on the victims. What I can tell you is Olive has two deep wounds, possibly from a knife. Mr. Robinson was hit repeatedly by something smaller, possibly an axe or hatchet. I'd say this attack was personal. Can't imagine anyone taking that much time to beat anyone. They would've been dead after the first few blows. I don't envy you this one."

Hodgins sighed as he looked across the room at the two covered bodies. "How could anyone hate so much?" Hodgins shook his head. "Good evening, Doctor." He glanced one last time at the bodies before leaving.

* * *

Hodgins' walk home was slow. The images of the battered family wouldn't leave his mind. There had been no word from the hospital about the two women yet. The distraction was so great he walked two blocks past his home before he noticed.

As soon as he entered the front door, Scraps raced down the hall to greet him. Hodgins pushed the dog away, rougher than he intended. Scraps whined. Hodgins didn't react, too wrapped up in the case. He hung his overcoat on the closest hook, went into the front room, and poured a large whisky.

Cordelia left the kitchen to check on the distressed dog. As she comforted Scrap, she spotted her husband by the fireplace and joined him.

"Whatever is the matter, Bertie? Scraps is sitting in the hall whimpering and I find you with a rather large glass of whisky. You only have that when my father visits."

He set the glass on the mantle, turned, and gave Cordelia a strong hug. "It was horrible, Delia. Worst I've seen."

She wiggled out of his grasp and led him to the settee. "Sit. Tell me what happened."

Hodgins slumped beside his wife, then suddenly looked up. "Where are the children?"

"In the back garden." She placed a hand on his arm when she saw the concerned look on his face. "They're fine. What's wrong? You're frightening me."

"There was another murder." He got up and retrieved his drink, swallowing half of it.

"Murder is your job. Why has this one upset you so?"

Hodgins downed the rest of the whisky and poured another. "Not just one murder. A young bride-to-be and her father. Mother and aunt are unconscious in the hospital. A baby and three young boys with their family torn apart. At least they were spared injury. All I could think about was you and the girls. If anything ever happened to any of you, I don't know what I'd do."

* * *

For the first time Hodgins could recall, he dreaded going to work. How could anyone be so cruel as to kill and injure so many? If someone had a grudge against Mr. Robinson, or any other member of the family, why not simply kill that person? What could anyone gain by harming others in the family?

Hodgins trudged to the station despite the drizzling, freezing rain. Too upset to take the streetcar, he simply turned up the collar of his overcoat and kept his head down. He didn't even take note of the horses clomping by.

At the station, before doing anything else, Hodgins made a cup of tea and lingered by the pot-belly stove. The wind and rain had chilled him to the bone. No matter how hot the weather, they kept a fire lit for tea. Slightly warmer, he went into his office and hung his overcoat on the hook.

Two sheets of paper on his desk caught Hodgins' attention. Before he left the night before, he'd put everything away. He recognized the writing; reports from Barnes and Riddell. He picked up the one from Barnes.

Hodgins mumbled as he read the information. "What did you find, Henry? Something of use, I hope."

As he read each report, he jotted items of interest on a fresh piece of paper. His list was short.

- *A broken fire poker in the parlour, no mention of blood on it*

- *A pile of filthy clothing in the main bedroom, along with a pair of boots with holes in the soles*

- *Dresser drawers pulled out*

- *Single playing card*

Hodgins circled the playing card. *Why only one?* Neither Barnes nor Riddell had made mention of a card set, so where did it come from? Nothing at the house had been removed except the bodies. *Time for another look.* He checked Barnes' and Riddell's desks, looking for the house key before heading out.

The rain had stopped by the time he left, and the walk to the murder scene was short and slippery. He entered the house and locked the door to prevent interruptions. First stop was the parlour. Blood stains on the carpet told him where one woman had been bludgeoned. The fire poker lay a few inches away. It appeared clean, but if it hadn't been used on the victim, why didn't it hang beside the fireplace with the rest of the set?

He picked it up and moved to a window for a better look. Not a speck of soot on it. *Someone must have cleaned it recently.* The fireplace hearth was clean. If Miss Shore was scrubbing it for the wedding, where was the rag? He placed the poker by the front door to take to the coroner, then went back in to check the game table. Hodgins had a similar one, but not as fancy. The Robinson family wasn't poor, but they couldn't afford something so elaborate. All the furniture appeared high quality.

Hodgins noticed initials engraved on the edge of the table—*JR*—Jacob Robinson. Based on the table, he'd been an excellent carpenter. He opened the drawer and pulled out two boxes. One contained checker pieces, the other chess. No cards. Just as Barnes said.

Next, Hodgins went into the family room. The roll-top desk sat near the front window, the clouds creating odd shapes on it from the sunlight peeking through. Barnes had provided details of the contents in every drawer except the locked one, so Hodgins didn't give it more than a glance. Nothing seemed out of place, so he went upstairs.

Olive's bedroom hadn't been disturbed. The stained sheets and blood splatter were the only indication of wrong-doing.

He continued on to Mr. and Mrs. Robinson's bedroom. The bed sat unmade. *Did she hear something and get up? Mrs. Robinson made it downstairs, but her room has been ransacked.* The wardrobe door was open, the pile of dirty clothes lay in front. He made a mental note to send Riddell back to collect them later.

Hodgins picked up the boots, noticing the holes. *Strange.* Nothing else in the house needed repair, and the clothing in the wardrobe appeared well-kept. He put the boots down headed out of the room. He stopped at the doorway and turned back. Mrs. Robinson had been found in the sewing room. He pulled his notebook from his pocket and made notes, then continued to the room across the hall.

Three small beds sat in a row against the far wall. The room was void of blood. Whatever happened didn't wake them. As Hodgins turned to leave, the clouds parted, and the sunlight glinted against something under the bed. Hodgins knelt down and reached under, pulling out a bloody knife. *Did the killer come in, then change his mind?* He found a pillowcase in the linen closet and placed the knife inside, then went downstairs and put the poker in with it. He didn't want to distress any passers-by when carrying them over to the coroner.

***

After dropping the items off with Stonehouse, Hodgins went back to the station.

"Barnes. Riddell. My office. Bring your notebooks." Hodgins placed his book beside the two reports. Barnes came in and sat in the chair in front of the desk. Riddell carried one in for himself.

"I've just been back to the house. It needs a more thorough go-through. We were all in shock yesterday and missed things."

He held up his hand before either constable could speak. "I'm not blaming anyone. It was a horrific sight." He looked at Riddell. "Find something for the boots and clothes in Mr. Robinson's bedroom. A sack will do. There's something not right about them, but I can't put my finger on it."

Hodgins tapped his notebook. "I found a bloody knife under one of the beds in the children's room. Only noticed it because the sun came out and hit the blade. I've taken it and the fire poker to the coroner."

"The poker?" Riddell cocked his head, puzzled. "But it was clean."

"Exactly. Too clean. If… what is the name of Mrs. Robinson's sister? If she was cleaning, where's the rag?"

"Miss Shore," Barnes said. "The sister's name is Catherine Shore."

"I want both of you working exclusively on this. Barnes, find out what else you can from the neighbours. There must be someone who knows everyone's business. Riddell, scour the house from top to bottom, then the yard, and Mr. Robinson's work shed. Take the clothing, and anything else unusual, to Stonehouse. And make note of what you find and the exact location."

CHAPTER FIVE

Barnes stood on the top step of the station house waiting for Riddell. He turned when the door opened. "What took you so long?"

"Thought I'd better grab a couple of extra sacks, just in case we find anything important." Constable Riddell held them up. "Found these in the rubbish out back. Richardson was about to burn them."

"Good thinking. We'd best get moving. I know the detective said he didn't blame anyone for missing the knife and leaving the poker, but we messed up."

They started towards the house, their steps slowing as they approached the curve on Wilton Street.

Riddell mumbled something.

"What was that, Tom? Speak up."

"I said sorry about making fun of you when you found the children. Must've been a terrible shock after seeing their sister. Can't imagine what went through your mind."

Barnes dismissed it with a wave of his hand and continued on. "You already apologized. I know everyone makes fun of me because of how I react at some scenes. Can't help it."

Riddell placed a hand on Barnes' shoulder. "You're a caring soul, Henry. The older coppers, they're hardened to everything. Don't ever think less of yourself because you care about people."

Barnes felt his face grow warm, and before he could reply, Riddell stopped.

"We're here. Let's do this right, even if it takes the rest of the day. When you finish with the neighbours, you come help me."

As they walked up the porch steps, someone called out. "Officers! Wait."

They turned and watched as a neighbour rushed across her lawn. "My husband told me to mind my own business, but I have to tell you."

Riddell jabbed Barnes with his elbow and whispered. "If you're lucky, all the neighbours will come to you. Save some boot leather." He continued up the steps and unlocked the door, leaving Barnes to start his part of their task.

Barnes beckoned her to the porch, where they could stand out of the snow. Now, you live in which house, and what's your name?

"I live at number sixty-eight with my husband, Hans. I'm Caroline Mueller and I think I saw the killer."

Barnes' eyebrows shot up. "You saw him? What did he look like?"

"I was in the garden, picking the last of the carrots and sprouts, and I heard a noise. I peeked through the hydrangea bush and saw him. Young man, same age as Olive, I think. Peering through the window."

Barnes wrote as she spoke. "What did he look like? Hair colour? How tall?"

"Oh, I didn't see his face, and he wore a cap. He was crouched down, peeking over the sill."

Barnes sighed. "So, you saw a man peeping through a window, but can't tell me what he looked like. What time was this?"

She scrunched her face in thought. "Just after luncheon. Maybe two o'clock."

"I don't believe that's our man. Too early in the day." He noticed the disappointed look on her face. "But you may have spotted a peeper. I'll let the neighbours know and we'll keep an eye out for him. Thank you."

She nodded, proud to have helped, then scurried home.

"A murderer and a peeper," Barnes muttered as he started for the next house. He got part way up the walkway and stopped. *Maybe the peeper was checking out the house and came back later and killed them? Maybe another person saw him?*

None of the occupants in the next few houses saw or heard anything, and he'd reached the end of the block. Barnes crossed the road and spoke with the neighbours across from the Robinson's. Everyone had the same reply. They saw nothing, heard nothing. When he reached the next block, he crossed back and checked with the people on the west side of Pembroke. The woman three up at number thirty-three saw a young man mid-afternoon.

"Did you get a look at his face, Mrs. McAvoy?"

"Oh, yes. He stopped and chatted for a few minutes. Said he knew Olive, but no one answered the door. I told him they were probably just busy preparing for the wedding. Said his name was George."

"You've not seen him around before?"

"No, and I'd remember him. Flaming red hair, mutton chops, and the deepest voice I've ever heard."

"Thank you, Mrs. McAvoy. That's quite helpful. Mrs. Mueller spotted a peeper about the same time. Keep your shades drawn at night.

No one answered their door on the rest of the block. Only two people in the area saw the red-haired man. *How could someone attack a family and no one hear anything?* He shoved his notebook into his pocket hard enough to pop a few stitches. "Dang."

He hurried up the Robinson's porch. Riddell had left the door unlocked, but the key still sat in the lock. Barnes turned the key after closing the door and left it on the side table just inside.

"Tom?"

"Upstairs. Just getting the dirty clothing and boots."

Barnes joined him in the Robinson's bedroom. "Got a description of a peeper. Might be the murderer. Did you find anything new?"

"Yes. Found something in Olive's room. Not sure if it's important, but…"

Riddell reached into his pocket, pulling out several letters. "Love letters, and not from Mr. Wright. I read a couple, and it sounds like she either didn't reply or simply rejected him. Unfortunately, they're from a post office box."

"We should be able to get a name from the post office. Where were they?"

"Found them in a box in her wardrobe."

"Why would she keep them if she spurned him? Especially as she's about to be wed?"

Riddell smiled. "Perhaps she liked the idea someone other than her betrothed fancied her?"

"You're probably right." Barnes looked around the room. "Are you finished in here?"

Riddell nodded. "Need to check the yard and the workshop. Which do you want?"

"I'll take the shop. Can't imagine the detective missed anything, but he wants us to go over the entire property."

Riddell picked up the sack, and they headed downstairs. He placed the letters on the small table just inside the front door beside the key and dropped the sack of clothing in front of it before they exited out the kitchen door.

Barnes walked over to the workshop. When he opened the door, a blast of heat hit him, causing him to step back. With everything closed up tight, the sun beating down on the roof heated the small building, despite the snow on the ground. "Is it too late to switch, Tom? It's hotter than the blacksmith's in there."

"You chose it."

Barnes groaned and moved a rock to hold the door open, then propped open the window. He hung his uniform jacket on a nail in the wall. It didn't take long for the chilly air to cool the workshop to a comfortable temperature.

One by one, Barnes examined the tools, using a lantern for more light. None of them had blood on them. They were far enough away from where Mr. Robinson had been killed that the splatter couldn't reach them. He left that area for last.

With nothing else to check, he moved towards where Mr. Robinson had been found. Even though Hodgins had already shifted the sacks, Barnes picked up each one, moving them after careful examination. Eventually, the pile sat a few feet from the bloodied area. Barnes found nothing hidden among them.

Barnes closed the windows, then moved the rock and closed the door. He saw Riddell at the back of the property and walked over as he shrugged into his uniform jacket, buttoning it tight around his neck.

"Find anything? Workshop's clean."

"Over here."

Barnes sped up and looked where Riddell pointed. Someone had hidden a bloody forge hammer and axe under the shrubbery.

"Hold the sack and I'll put them in." Riddell handed an empty sack to Barnes, then picked up the tools. "Good thing I brought extra."

"Whoever did this was mighty angry. An unfinished table leg, knife, hammer, and axe. I don't think he came intending to kill anyone. Everything's from the house or workshop." Barnes wound the top of the sack around his fist. "Better get this to the coroner, then let Hodgins know."

CHAPTER SIX

Once the items had been dropped off at the coroner's, the constables returned to the station and headed straight for Hodgins' office.

"Sir, you won't believe what we found—"

"Never thought to look under the bushes. Can't believe—"

The detective waved his hands. "Slow down. Speak one at a time. Barnes, you first."

"Let Tom do the talking. They're his discoveries."

"Fine. Riddell, what did you find?"

"Love letters, an axe, and a forge hammer. Hidden under a bush. The axe and hammer, I mean. The letters were in a box in Olive's wardrobe." Riddell handed the letters to Hodgins. "Rest of the things are with Dr. Stonehouse."

Barnes leaned forward, pointing to the letters. "Spurned admirer. Do you think he went funny in the head after she rejected him?

Hodgins grinned. "Love can do strange things to people. Not certain he'd try to kill her family, though."

He opened one and read it. "Nothing threatening. Corresponding through a postal box. Riddell, you found the items, so write up a detailed report. Barnes, see what you can find out from the post office."

Riddell left, but Barnes lingered. "Sir, there are two ladies who said they saw a man yesterday afternoon. One was peeping through the Robinson's window. Don't know if both sightings were the same man or not. Red hair, mutton chops, and about Olive's age."

Hodgins twisted the end of his mustache. "A peeper? Interesting. I'll speak with her fiancé and see if he recognizes the description. Now, off with you. When you return, write up your report, starting with your inquires with the neighbours."

* * *

With the lads busy, Hodgins went to the Wright residence to question Samuel. He rapped on the door several times before Mrs. Wright answered it.

"Excuse the intrusion. Might I have a word with your son? Something has turned up in our inquiries."

She stepped aside and allowed him entry, pointing to the side room. "He's in the sitting room. Please, be brief."

"Yes ma'am. Thank you."

Hodgins found Sam with his father, both sitting by the fire. "I'm afraid I have a few more questions. Won't take long. Do you have any friends with red hair and mutton chops? School chum perhaps?"

Sam Wright shook his head. "Not many my age wear mutton chops. They're for old men."

"What about Olive? Did she know anyone like that? A relative perhaps?"

Another shrug. "No one I've met."

Hodgins tapped his notebook. "You don't know anyone with red hair? No one at all? Passing acquaintance? Shopkeeper?"

"Sorry. Wish I could… wait. There is someone, but he moved away several years ago."

Hodgins opened his notebook. "What's his name? Do you know where he moved to?"

"I should have his address, but he may have moved again." Sam got up, opened the hinged panel on the secretary desk, and rooted through it.

"His father changed jobs frequently. Finally had to leave the city. Not a bad fellow, just not especially good at anything." He held up an envelope. "Here it is. We lost touch. Last I heard from him, they lived in Newmarket." He returned to Hodgins and handed him the envelope.

"Twelve Lydia Street." Hodgins copied it down. "Mr. George Franklin. If he was in town, wouldn't he have looked you up?"

"You said he was seen the afternoon before—" His voice caught. "Forgive me. If it was George, maybe he planned to call the next day, heard the news, and changed his mind. We were close growing up, but had little contact once his family left the city."

A slight smile crossed Sam's face. "Everyone, the boys, that is, were sweet on Olive. Some of the girls were jealous. My friends congratulated me when she agreed to allow me to court her. Everyone except George. Quite jealous, he was, but he got over it."

"Maybe not," Hodgins mumbled under his breath. He made a couple of notes, then stood. "Thank you for your time."

* * *

Hodgins sat at his desk the next morning, staring at his notes. He'd read them numerous times, hoping something stood out. He began scribbling on a fresh sheet of paper. Only three items sat at the top of the page: peeper, red hair, jealousy.

"Morning, sir." Barnes stood in the doorway, notebook in hand.

Hodgins waved him in. "Sit. Go over this with me." He slid the nearly blank piece of paper across the desk. "Are the red-haired man and the peeper one and the same? Mr. Wright remembered a red-haired friend from childhood who'd been sweet on Olive. Could he be the person the neighbour spoke to? Could it be that simple?"

Barnes held up his notebook. "When I interviewed the neighbour to the east of Robinson's, she didn't say anything about the peeper having red hair. Said he wore a hat, but if he had mutton chops, she'd have seen them, even if she couldn't make out the color."

"Good point. Unless he shaved them off. What time was he seen? You said the other neighbour saw the red-head in the afternoon."

Barnes searched through his notes. "Here it is. She thought it was around two."

"So, unless he carried a razor in his pocket, they aren't the same man. I'll head up to Newmarket to try to track down Mr. Wright's old friend, George Franklin." Hodgins retrieved his much-used Northern Railway schedule and spread it on his desk. "Think I'd have this memorized by now. Looks like I've missed the first train. I can make the 1:07 p.m. I'll have plenty of time to find out if Mr. Franklin is still there and to have a chat with him. Nice not to rush or stay overnight. Just hope this old address is good."

"Still need to check on that post office box. I'll do that right away." Barnes' eyebrows shot up. "I just realized. You said the man you're looking for is Mr. Franklin. He signed the letters Frankie. Could that be a nickname?"

"Bit of a stretch, but anything's possible. Where's Riddell?"

Barnes leaned back, grinning. "Went to check on Mrs. Shore, Mrs. Robinson's mother. See if she needs anything more for little Susie. He seems quite taken with the baby. He'll also see if she knows of anyone with a grudge or knows about the letters."

"I want you to follow up on Simmons' claim about playing cards at his home that night. See if anyone else was there, what time they arrived and left. Talk to them all and ask about George Franklin and Frankie. Find out if they're the same person."

Barnes jotted everything down and headed out.

***

Neither Barnes nor Riddell had returned by the time Hodgins left for Union Station. For once, he wasn't rushed, allowing him time to sit at the train station reading the newspaper.

When the train pulled in, he assisted a woman travelling alone with a baby and an enormous steamer trunk. He sat chatting with her for the entire ride. When he exited at Newmarket, she continued north.

One of the porters at the station provided directions to Lydia Street. The walk took longer than expected because of the early fall heatwave, but Hodgins arrived at his destination in less than a half hour. Mrs. Franklin answered the door dressed entirely in black.

"I'm sorry to intrude. I wasn't aware there'd been a death in the family." He showed his badge. Is this the Franklin residence? I need to speak with George.

"Come in. My husband passed several months ago. It's just Georgie and me. I'm afraid he's not home at the moment. Is there something I can help you with?" She led him into the kitchen. "Tea?"

"Thank you. There's been a murder in Toronto. An old acquaintance of your son's. Olive Robinson."

The tea cups clattered as she dropped them on the table. Hodgins grabbed one that headed towards the edge, then guided her to a chair. "I'm sorry to be so abrupt. Let me pour the tea."

Once they were both seated, he opened his notebook. "From your reaction, can I assume you remember Olive?"

"Yes. We lived down the street from them for several years. I must write a condolence letter to her parents at once."

Hodgins reached across the table and placed a hand over hers. "I'm afraid Mrs. Robinson is in the hospital. Mr. Robinson is dead."

Mrs. Franklin fell face down on the table in a dead faint.

"Damn. Should have got someone to sit with her first." Hodgins continued berating himself while trying to revive her. He struggled to get her hefty form off the table and leaning back against the chair, but she hadn't come to. He hurried to the sink and pumped water to wet a cloth.

"Hello? June?" A woman stood at the back door and knocked. Before Hodgins could respond, the door opened, and she came in. "June, why didn't you answer?"

"Excuse me." Hodgins stepped away from the sink and into view of the woman.

She jumped. "Who are you?" She looked at Mrs. Franklin, finally realizing she wasn't conscience. "What have you done?" She edged around the table.

Hodgins pulled out his badge. "She fainted. Afraid I gave her some bad news."

The woman examined his badge, then relaxed. "I'm Bea. Live next door."

"Would you mind helping me get her to a more comfortable chair? Maybe send for a doctor? She fell forward and banged her head. Bump's already beginning to rise."

Bea took the wet cloth and held it against Mrs. Franklin's forehead. "Has something happened to George?"

"No. An old acquaintance. Didn't think she'd take it so hard."

"She's not what you'd call delicate, but ever since her husband died, well, she takes things harder."

Mrs. Franklin came around, moaning slightly. They got her on her feet and into the small family room, then onto an over-stuffed, well-used chair. Hodgins looked around. The furnishings were quite worn, but clean and expertly repaired.

"Where might I find her son?"

"He works at the Borland and Roe Hotel, but he's out of town at the moment. Left day before yesterday."

Hodgins reached into his pocket for his notebook, then realized he'd left it on the kitchen table. "Do you know when he'll be back?"

"No. June's in no condition to answer your questions. I think you should leave."

"Yes, ma'am. I'll just…" He pointed to the kitchen. Her glare told him she wasn't about to argue with him. "Forgot something." He raced to the kitchen, grabbed his notebook, and practically ran out the front door. He looked back to see Bea standing at the window.

A young woman approached, pushing a pram. She glanced at the house. "I see you've met Bea."

"Yes, she's quite, um, forthright."

"Pushy, more like."

Bea hollered out the open window. "Gertie, fetch the doctor. Now." She disappeared from view.

"A doctor? Has something happened to June?"

"She fainted and banged her head."

"Oh, my." She turned around and scampered off, leaving Hodgins looking around, trying to determine which way to go.

He checked the time on his pocket watch. Plenty of time to catch the train. He hadn't asked where the hotel was, but wasn't going back to Mrs. Franklin's to find out. He walked down the street and saw the young woman with the baby speaking to a man, who then raced off. Hodgins called to the woman.

"Could you direct me to the Borland?"

"Yes, cross the railway tracks and go to Main Street. Just a few blocks north."

CHAPTER SEVEN

He found the hotel easily. It served two purposes for Hodgins. A place to wait until the train arrived, and an opportunity to ask about George Franklin. As it was an unusually hot day, instead of his usual tea, Hodgins ordered a beer. When the server returned with it, he asked about George, not identifying himself as a police officer.

"Looking for a friend. George Franklin. Understand he works here."

The server grunted. "Ya, but he ain't here. Wrangled a few days off."

"Only a few days? So he'll be back soon? Don't suppose you know where I might find him?"

"I ain't his keeper. Come back next week." He turned to wipe the next table.

Hodgins spoke to the man's back. "Tell me, does he still wear those bushy mutton chops?"

"Not since he's worked here." The server wandered off without giving Hodgins so much as a glance.

Hodgins downed half his beer, then jotted in his notebook. At least he discovered the man the Robinson's neighbour spoke to wasn't Franklin. That left the peeper and the author of the love letters. Hodgins hadn't eaten since breakfast and wouldn't arrive home until after the evening meal, so he ordered a ploughman's lunch and another beer.

An hour before the train arrived, he began the walk to the station. Unlike the ride up, he spoke to no one on the way home and went straight to the station to see if Barnes or Riddell were around. When he entered his office, two new reports sat on his desk.

Riddell's report mentioned a brief discussion with Mrs. Robinson's mother. She knew about the love letters, but not who wrote them. Barnes' report didn't fare any better. The post office box had been paid in cash by Mr. C. Dickens. Hodgins chuckled at the probably fake name, wondering if Barnes got the joke. The description of the man renting the post office box matched what he knew about Franklin. He initialed both reports and left them on Riddell's and Barnes' desks to file, then headed home.

Hodgins was exhausted, mostly because of the heatwave, so he flagged a hansom for the trip home. When he opened the front door, Scraps walked down the hall to greet him.

No jumping tonight. Simply a soft woof. Hodgins reached down to scratch the dog's head.

"Must be extra bad for you with all that fur. Please tell me you don't need a walk."

"He's been taken care of." Delia stood at the end of the hall. "Sara took him around the block before we ate. Just a simple cold meal tonight. Plenty of leftovers."

Hodgins waved the comment off. "Ate earlier up in Newmarket. Join me in the front parlour?"

Scraps followed Hodgins and laid on the rug in front of the unlit fireplace. Hodgins sat in the chair beside it. Delia came in soon after with two glasses of lemonade. She handed one to her husband, then sat in the matching chair.

Hodgins leaned back and closed his eyes. Soft scuffling sounds drifted down the stairs, along with Sara's voice, as she spoke to the twins. After a few minutes, he finally spoke.

"We've got a few leads, but haven't been able to confirm anything. How could someone murder and injure four people and no one see or hear anything?"

Delia sipped her lemonade before speaking. "Why don't you tell me what you have? When you talk it out, something generally clicks into place."

He grinned. "After a careful observation by you most times. We have one suspect we can't positively identify and one who might be the person we're looking for."

He took his notebook from his pocket but didn't open it. "Did I tell you about the love letters?"

When Delia shook her head, he filled her in on the details. "So, the question is, is George Franklin Frankie? Barnes checked the post office. The box was rented by Mr. C. Dickens."

"So it's not—Oh. Charles Dickens. How clever. But not helpful. Did you find Mr. Franklin?"

"No. He's conveniently out of town. Couldn't get much from his mother. She fainted when I told her about the murders. Banged her head." Hodgins described the encounter with the neighbour, Bea. "She'd be quite a match for your mother."

Delia giggled. "And you ran off like a scared rabbit?"

Hodgins straightened in the chair. "No. I did not run off. Mrs. Franklin wasn't in any condition to answer any further questions. I simply decided to go to Franklin's place of employment and ask around." He looked at Delia, who grinned at him, then he slumped. "Fine. I ran off like a scared rabbit. I'll head back next week. She should be sufficiently recovered, and Franklin should be back."

He guzzled the lemonade and stood, extending his hand to Delia. "I'm ready for more. Can I fill your glass?"

When he returned, Delia worked on her needlepoint. Hodgins checked the bookshelf and pulled out *The Chimes* by Charles Dickens and settled back in his chair.

CHAPTER EIGHT

When Hodgins woke the next morning, the heat of the last few days had subsided to more average late fall temperatures. A gentle breeze flowed through the bedroom window. He propped it all the way up, allowing more air in to cool the room.

Delia had already risen, the sounds of clattering dishes and pots downstairs alerting him to breakfast preparations. He dressed, then roused Sara and the twins. Once ready, Sara helped Ivy down the staircase. Hodgins took Holly.

He ate a quick meal, then began his forty-five-minute walk to the station. Hodgins wanted to review Barnes' discussions with Mrs. Simmons. She hadn't been able to confirm what time the young men were at the house playing cards the evening of the murder. He pulled the file and sat at Barnes' desk.

When Barnes arrived, Hodgins waved the report. "Can you elaborate on your talk with Mrs. Simmons? Why didn't she know when Wright and the rest were there?"

"Sorry, sir. I'll add to it. She went out before the lads all arrived. Dinner at a friend's. She remembers Sam Wright and Geoffrey Lockerby were there before she left, and they were gone when she returned."

"And her husband?"

"Working late. He's a lawyer."

Hodgins rose from Barnes' desk, leaving the report for Barnes to add to. "So, no one can confirm their alibis. Maybe the neighbours saw them? Something else has been bothering me. That playing card. You didn't find the rest of the cards at the Robinson house, so where the blazes did it come from?"

Barnes thought for a moment. "Maybe Mr. Robinson had company and someone else brought the deck? One could have fallen off the table and been missed when packing up."

Hodgins disagreed. "That house was spotless. Well, except for the blood. The card would've been discovered while cleaning. Someone must have dropped shortly it before the murder. Question is, did the murderer lose it? Is it an important clue?"

Hodgins looked over when the station door opened. "Riddell." He waved him over. "I want both of you to look into the lads that were playing cards with Wright. Talk to their neighbours and chums at school. See if they've been in trouble, no matter how trivial."

He moved towards his office, stopped, and turned back. "You two go to the school. I'll speak to their family and neighbours. Want to give Mrs. Franklin another day to recover. Hopefully, her son will have returned by then, too.

* * *

The first stop Hodgins made was at the Simmons' house. "Sorry to intrude, but I need to follow up on my constables' inquires." He introduced himself and Mrs. Simmons led him to the parlour.

"Ghastly what happened to the Robinsons. A person's not safe in their own home. I hope you plan on doing something about it." She waggled a finger in front of his face.

"We're doing everything we can. I'm trying to determine everyone's whereabouts that evening. Hoping someone was near the house and saw something. The quickest route between here and the Wright residence goes by the Robinsons. Do you know if Mr. Wright came by himself, or perhaps your son fetched him or one of the other lads?"

"Matthew was here, getting the card table set up. Let me think." She placed a finger on her chin, pursing her lips as she thought. "Sam arrived just as I was preparing to leave.

Geoffrey was with him, but I don't know if they came together, or simply arrived at the same time."

Hodgins made notes as she spoke. "Which one is Geoffrey?"

"The Lockerby boy."

"And they were gone when you returned?"

"Yes. Matthew was in bed."

"Thank you, Mrs. Simmons. I won't delay you further."

Hodgins left, then went to the closest neighbours to see if anyone saw the young men come or go. A few saw one or two arrive, but no one saw them leave. The neighbour to the west mentioned a ruckus and thought she heard a woman's voice.

He went to the Lockerby house next, wondering if poker was the only game they played that night. Mrs. Lockerby wasn't any more helpful than Mrs. Simmons was. The dinner engagement that evening was also a committee meeting for the church, attended by two of the other lad's mothers.

Nothing came from Hodgins' inquires except the possibility the young men enjoyed the company of a woman as well as playing cards. Assuming they actually bothered with the card game. Maybe they planned a little entertainment for the groom before he wed?

A few blocks from the station, a constable ran towards him.

"Sir, we've been looking all over for you."

"Catch your breath. What's so important you had to run around trying to find me? Couldn't it wait until I returned?"

"Constable Barnes sent us out looking. Said to tell you, Sam Wright's been found murdered on campus."

CHAPTER NINE

Hodgins flagged down the first hansom that passed and raced to the campus. The crowd by one building alerted Hodgins where he needed to go. Several constables tried holding back the students. A middle-aged man with an authoritative air stormed out of the building towards the throng of young men.

Within minutes, the crowd dissipated. Hodgins hurried over. He'd been able to hear the man's booming voice, but not well enough to make out the words. The man approached, meeting him half-way. Hodgins showed his badge and introduced himself.

"Not certain what you said, but thank you for clearing the students."

The man thrust out his hand. "McCaul. Principal here."

Hodgins noticed the Irish lilt. McCaul's eyes twinkled as he spoke. "Told the boys I'd expel them all if they didn't return to class." The twinkle disappeared as quickly as it appeared. "I heard what happened. Terrible, just terrible.

I've already started making preparations for a service here at our chapel on campus, for the students and staff.

Hodgins looked over McCaul's shoulder, noticing Barnes waving his arms. "I'm needed at the scene. Thank you again for clearing the students from underfoot." He rushed over to Barnes. "Please tell me the constable exaggerated and this is simply an accident."

"Sorry, but it's no accident." Barnes led Hodgins into a treed area. Stonehouse was already there, kneeling beside the body.

"Doctor, what can you tell me?"

Stonehouse knelt beside the body, glancing up at Hodgins. "Someone slit his throat. Not too deep, so it didn't kill him instantly. He likely fell, then the killer stabbed him numerous times. Won't be able to give you a count until I've got him cleaned up."

Hodgins looked down at the body of the young man. "Is it a coincidence someone attacked his fiancé and family, then the intended groom?" He looked around. "Where's Riddell?"

"Interviewing the two lads who found him. They were in quite a state. The headmaster gave them a room in the main building." Barnes pointed behind Hodgins. "On their way back now."

Hodgins turned to see the crowd gathering again. "Any of you know Wright?" A few nodded. "Stay put. The rest of you clear off or I'll get McCaul back out."

The crowd scattered, except the four who knew Wright. "McCaul that bad?"

"No," one student said. "He's tough, but fair. And very strict."

"Barnes, get your notebook out. Take down their names and addresses."

Once the details were provided, Hodgins questioned them. "Are you friends or just schoolmates with Wright?"

"We're all in several classes with him," the one wearing glasses said. "We don't socialize off campus." The other three nodded.

"Did any of you notice anything peculiar today? Or recently?"

Three heads shook *no*. The fourth student opened his mouth briefly, saying nothing.

"Out with it."

"I saw him arguing with someone earlier this morning. I was too far away to hear, but the other lad shoved Sam. They started fighting. Someone yelled that a teacher was coming and the other person shot off."

"Did you know who he fought with? Another student?"

"Never seen him before. I'd remember a student with bushy red mutton chops."

"Mutton chops again, sir." Barnes stopped scribbling in his notebook and looked at Hodgins. "Must be the same man the neighbour saw."

"Most likely. Anything else, boys?" They shrugged and shook their heads. "Off with you then." He turned and joined Stonehouse.

"Can I move the body now?" Stonehouse stood.

"Yes, Doctor. You can take him to the morgue."

"I'll bring my buggy closer. One of you can help load him."

A few minutes later, Stonehouse pulled his team to a halt near the trees. He jumped off and walked over. "I'll take his head. Who's taking his feet?

Hodgins stepped forward, but Barnes spoke up. "I'll do it." He glanced down at Wright's body and paled slightly, then bent down at grabbed the feet. When they lifted him, Hodgins spotted something underneath and grabbed it before it got trampled.

Once Stonehouse left, Hodgins slapped Barnes on the back. "That wasn't so bad, was it? Have you checked the area?"

"No, sir. What's that you've got there?"

Hodgins held out his hand, revealing a dark brown leather glove.

"Where did you find that, sir?"

"Under the body of Sam Wright. Only the one, and I didn't see the other on Wright's hand. Might be from the killer."

Barnes took the glove. "Soft leather, expensive looking. Our killer must have money."

CHAPTER TEN

Hodgins sat at his desk, the playing card laying on the desk in front of him. He ran his fingers over a tiny nick in the upper right corner. *Gambler's marked deck.* He called Barnes.

"Look at this." Hodgins handed the card to the constable. "What do you see?"

Barnes turned the card, examining both sides. "It's the queen of hearts."

He started to give the card back when he noticed. "Sir! It's marked." Barnes placed the card on the desk. "Would take a skilled cheat to feel the difference."

"Is there anyone on our list who's a gambler?"

"No, sir. Not that we've come across."

"You and Riddell check out the gambling dens. See if anyone recognizes the names or descriptions. Don't lean too hard and make certain they understand we're not interested in their business. We only want to find the murderer. I'm going back to the university to talk to those lads again. Hopefully, they've remembered something else."

When Hodgins arrived at the campus, he unfolded the schedules to see where he could locate Sam's friends. They all had a free period. "Blast. Could be anywhere," he muttered.

He thought back to his year studying law at Osgoode Hall and snapped his fingers. "Must be a study hall somewhere."

Hodgins stopped the first person he encountered and got directions. Unfortunately, the study hall only had a few students, none that he wanted. He approached the closest table.

"Excuse me." He kept his voice low. "By any chance do you know Lockerby, Adams, Gerrard, Simmons, or Thomms?"

Two shook their head, but the third nodded. "Don't know him well, but I know who Thomms is."

"Have you seen him today?"

"No, sorry."

"Hmm. Where else might one go for a free period?"

Three sets of shoulders shrugged.

"Unless…" The one student who vaguely knew Thomms hesitated.

"Go on."

"Every year the students put on a Christmas pantomime. They've already put up the post for actors. I think I saw Thomms' name on the list. He might be in the auditorium."

Hodgins made a quick note in his book. "Thank you. And the auditorium is…

One boy drew a sketch for Hodgins.

The dark-haired boy snickered. "Guess coppers don't see the inside of universities often."

Hodgins raised an eyebrow. "Not this one. I went to Osgoode."

Hodgins turned, but not before he saw all jaws drop open in surprise. It was common knowledge most of the force has little education. The map was easy to follow, and he found the auditorium quickly. Both Thomms and Lockerby were there. Hodgins settled in one of the back rows to watch.

A dozen students sat along the edge of the stage, trying to decide on the story. Half wanted to do St. George and the Dragon, and the other half argued for Bluebeard. Since the free period was almost over, Hodgins stood and approached. Lockerby noticed him first.

"Detective. Come to join us slay the dragon?" Lockerby grinned.

Hodgins smiled. "Have a dragon of my own to deal with. I'd like to have a word with you and Thomms before you rush off to class. About Sam."

The smile disappeared. "Yes. Sam."

Lockerby and Thomms hopped off the stage and joined Hodgins in the front row. The other boys sat listening.

"Do you know of anyone wishing Sam ill?" Hodgins looked at the lads on the stage. "Any of you?"

They all mumbled "no."

"Everyone who knew Sam took an instant liking to him." Thomms stood and paced. "Why would anyone want to kill him? Just doesn't make any sense."

Hodgins tapped the notebook with his pencil. "Someone saw a red-headed lad around the time of the attack. Can you think of anyone who matches that description? Mutton chops, too." He glanced at all the students.

"No."

"Sorry."

"What about gambling debts?" Hodgins glanced from one young man to the other.

Thomms laughed. "Sammy wasn't a gambler. When we played, it was generally for matchsticks. He had no vices that I know of. Straight as they come, old Sammy."

Lockerby nudged Thomms. "We've got to get going. If we're late for class again, Dunning will give us extra assignments and fail us if they're not up to snuff." He turned to Hodgins. "Got a dragon of our own."

The students rushed up the aisle and into the hall. A general commotion picked up as students moved from one class to another. Rather than track down the others, he headed back to the station. He remembered how important the first few months at school were. Set the wrong tone and the teacher would be on your back, likely until graduation, based on what his former classmates told him. He glanced into one of the class rooms. *Maybe I should have stayed at Osgoode and completed my law degree.*

When he returned to the station, Barnes got up from his desk and followed the detective.

"Sir, I may have found something. I went back to look through the desk again. Mr. Robinson's desk, that is. I'd only glanced at the invoices before. I found this." Barnes removed a piece of paper he'd tucked in his notebook and unfolded it. "Someone wasn't best pleased with him."

He handed the paper to Hodgins. "A threat? Or possibly someone just blowing off steam?" Hodgins skipped to the signature. "Have you found Mr. Tufford?"

"Not yet. I went to the address at the top of the stationery, but no one was home. One of his neighbours said he'd gone out of town on business. Apparently, he's a bachelor and has a temper. Not violent, though. Likes to hear himself talk, she said. Rather full of himself."

Hodgins read the letter in full. "Seems he was less than impressed with some furniture Robinson built. I saw his work at the house. He was an excellent woodworker. Mr. Tufford must be extremely picky. Find out what he does and when he's expected back. Talk to his associates and more of his neighbours. And friends, if he has any. It's a long shot, but someone was angry or unstable enough to bludgeon half the family."

"Yes, sir. Do you know what will become of the baby and boys?"

"She'll stay with her grandmother. Mrs. Shore might take the boys, too, but being a widow and a little elderly, she might not be able to handle a baby and four growing lads. At least they have family, regardless of who raises them. Assuming Mrs. Robinson and her sister don't survive."

Barnes got up, but didn't leave.

"Something on your mind constable?"

"What would make a person do so much damage to one family? He must not be right in the head."

"Yes. It's not something we come across often. Hopefully never again. Possibly the work of a madman or someone who just snapped. If he was after Mr. Robinson, why go into the house and murder Olive and attack his wife and her sister? His work shed is far enough from the house that none of the family would know anything was happening."

"Exactly. Has anyone escaped from the asylum?"

Hodgins chuckled. "No. I think we'd have heard about that by now. I believe it has to be someone known to the family. Find out what you can about Tufford. Now, what have you done with Riddell?"

"Following up on something we found out at one of the gambling dens. Seems Thomms and Lockerby both like to gamble. He's gone to the bank to check on their finances."

An unexpected racket at the front of the station house interrupted Barnes' report. The front door slammed, and they heard someone running. Riddell slid to a stop at Hodgins' door, panting.

"Sir." He took a few deep breaths. "Thomms."

Barnes moved the chair from in front of Hodgins' desk closer to the door. "Sit down, Tom. Catch your breath."

"When I left the bank, one of the fellows from the gambling den in The Junction was waiting for me. Said they'd banned Thomms for cheating at cards."

"The card!" Barnes turned to Hodgins. "Thomms must be the killer."

Hodgins still had the card on his desk and picked it up. "Would he be so cocky as to leave such an obvious clue?"

He checked the time. "He should be leaving his last class soon. Fetch him here, Barnes. Let's see what he has to say for himself."

CHAPTER ELEVEN

Hodgins sat in the interview room with Thomms, the playing card on the table. "I understand you like to gamble. Got in over your head?"

Thomms leaned back, legs crossed like he was chatting with a friend. "I enjoy a good game of cards with my friends. Nothing more."

"So you don't have any outstanding debts or problems in The Junction?"

The cocky look on Thomms' face faltered. "The Junction?"

"Yes. We've heard you owe a considerable sum." Hodgins guessed he'd probably lost a lot of money if he'd resorted to cheating in front of professionals. "Got caught cheating, too. I don't imagine they thought too highly of that. Cuts into their profits."

He held up the card. "This wouldn't belong to a deck of your own cards, would it?" He fingered the notched corner. "Specially marked. Get caught trying to switch decks?"

Thomms regained his composure and straightened in the chair. "I don't know what you're talking about. I've never seen that before. If you go around telling people I've been gambling and cheating, I'll sue you and the department for defamation of character. Matthew's father is a lawyer, you know. He'll help me. Crooked coppers, the lot of you. On the take."

Hodgins smiled. "Defamation of character, lad. Goes both ways. We can't connect this card to you. Not yet anyway. You're free to go, but if you need to leave town, let us know."

Hodgins remained in the room for a few minutes, trying to figure out a way to connect the card to Thomms, or anyone. He went back to his office and waved Barnes and Riddell in.

"Were any of the people at the gambling houses helpful? Riddell, that chap that waited at the bank, maybe? I need to know if there's anyone in particular that makes marked cards."

Riddell scratched his head. "Not sure where to find him, but I can put the word out."

"Good. Make it clear you have no intention of arresting the man. He helps us and we turn a blind eye. It takes a good eye and steady hand to make cuts this small and precise. Even if he doesn't know his name, he may recognize the lad's description. Hopefully, there aren't many Thomms' age looking for cheating aids. Forgot to ask. What did you find out about his finances?"

"Nothing yet. Only got to one bank, the St. Lawrence Bank, before that chap from the gambling house stopped me. Adams has an account there, and it's what you'd expect for a student. Monthly deposits from his father. Balance down to a few dollars by the time daddy's payment is deposited."

"Wish I had someone to make monthly deposits into my account. With three children and a dog, my pay doesn't go far." Hodgins crossed his fingers under his desk, hoping no one knew about his investments and large payouts.

"Barnes, you check the other banks while Riddell is looking for his contact. If he does actually owe money, he may have applied for a loan. He couldn't very well ask his father to bail him out, unless they're both gamblers. He definitely wouldn't want it getting back to the university. Probably get him expelled. I know when I was at Osgoode, even the smallest discretion would earn you the boot."

Hodgins checked his pocket watch. "It's getting late. Riddell, have a quick look around for your snitch, then call it a night. Barnes, I'll try to find Mr. Tufford in the morning while you make the rounds at the banks.

* * *

When Hodgins arrived home that evening, the house was unusually quiet. Sara was old enough not to be racing around, but the twins recently began walking. Scraps would run circles around them, barking and occasionally knocking things over. Cordelia had made sure the breakables were safe from the commotion.

As soon as he opened the front door, he smiled, inhaling deep. Pot roast, and it wasn't even Sunday. He went down the hall, stopping at the kitchen door. Beneath her apron, Cordelia wore her best dress. *Am I forgetting an important date?*

"Good evening, Delia." Hodgins moved up behind her, causing her to jump. He worded his question carefully, not wanting to alert his wife to his failing memory. "Where are the children? Sara should be helping you."

"Gracious, I didn't hear you come in." She wiped her hands and kissed him. "Mother and Father came over unexpectedly and said they were taking them and Scraps for a couple of days. Mother seems to think we need some time alone. I could hardly decline the offer."

"Surprised they took the dog. Your mother isn't fond of him."

"I don't believe they planned on taking Scraps, but he made such a fuss when they got in the buggy, and then twins began to cry. Surprised the neighbours didn't complain at the racket. Father said they'd take him, despite Mother's protests. Now, go change while I'm finishing dinner."

Hodgins put on his Sunday best and set the dining room table when he came back down. They normally ate in the kitchen, except on the rare occasion they had company. He got the good China out and even placed the sterling silver candelabrum on the table. When Cordelia brought their meal in, he lit the candles.

"We haven't done this since, well, never." Cordelia cocked her head, thinking. "Why haven't we ever done this?"

"That's easy. We were living with your parents until recently. They never socialized, so we've not had time alone, unless we went out for a meal and they watched Sara. Since we were in a restaurant full of people, we still weren't alone."

They ate in silence, occasionally chatting about the weather. Cordelia finally gave in. "Tell me more about these murders. What have you found out? Do you have any suspects?"

"A romantic evening with my lovely wife and we have nothing to talk about except corpses? We'll have to work on that." He gave a soft chuckle. "We have a few people we're looking into. A student, an old neighbour, and a disgruntled customer. Unfortunately, we have nothing definite on any of them."

"I remember. You were up in Newmarket looking for the lad that went to school with the eldest daughter and her fiancé. Did you ever locate him?"

Hodgins shook his head. "No. I have to go back again. He must have returned by now. Tomorrow, I need to locate the man who sent a threatening letter to Mr. Robinson, complaining about some work he did. Seems he's out of town as well, but there must be friends or family around."

"It almost sounds like everyone is avoiding you." She cleared their plates and returned from the kitchen with a steaming Apple Charlotte.

Hodgins licked his lips, eyeing the dessert. "My, you have outdone yourself today. Your parents deserve a reward for emptying the house. I'm afraid I've been negligent with my attention to you."

"It's nice to be appreciated. And you have not been neglectful. Now, tell me about this student. Why do you suspect one so young?"

"He's an old school mate of two of the deceased. A long-time friend. Did I tell you about the leather glove left under Wright's body and the card found at the Robinson's?"

Delia shook her head.

"The card belongs to a marked deck. It turns out this lad, Thomms, has frequented a gambling den up in The

Junction. Even got himself tossed for cheating. We can't link the card to him yet, but I've got Riddell on it."

"And the love letters? I still believe that's the key. I'm certain you'll find out this is all about love."

"Jealousy? Maybe. It's definitely a better reason than a botched furniture job." He pushed his empty dessert plate away. "Splendid meal, as always. Now, how about we spend the rest of the evening on more intimate things?"

* * *

The next morning Hodgins arrived at the station a little later than usual. Sergeant Cooper stopped him as he passed his desk.

"Sir, we've been waiting for you. Got word a little while ago. Riddell's in the hospital. Worked over pretty good, by all accounts. Someone found him in an alley. Barnes has already gone over."

"Good Lord." Hodgins headed back out and hailed the first cabriolet he saw.

When he entered the hospital room, memories of his attack in the alley beside the station, over a year ago, flashed through his head. The bruising and swelling made Riddell almost unrecognizable.

Barnes looked up, putting his finger to his lips. "Shh. He's sleeping. Tom came to a little while ago, but the doctor gave him something for the pain. Harrington went to fetch Tom's mum."

"Does anyone know what happened to him? Who found him?"

"He wasn't conscious long enough to say anything. One of the street girls found him. She's a regular on Tom's beat. He doesn't give the girls a hard time, so she flagged down a cab rather than leaving him there bleeding. Turns out the driver also knows Tom, so he carried him into his buggy and brought him here, no charge."

"Nice to know there are still people in the city who help one another. A street girl, eh? The driver know her name?"

"Didn't say. I gave him two bits for his time, though."

Hodgins clapped Barnes on the shoulder. "Good of you. I wonder if this has anything to do with him looking for the gambling snitch?"

A woman entered the room, interrupting their conversation. She let out a scream and fainted. Fortunately, Hodgins was close enough to catch her.

"Barnes, the chair. Must be Mrs. Riddell."

A nurse rushed in.

"It's all right, Sister. Understandable reaction, seeing her son like that. Don't suppose the doctor is around?" Hodgins showed his badge. "I'd like to speak with him."

"He's with another patient. I'll let him know you're waiting." She looked at Mrs. Riddell. "If she needs smelling salts, I'll be at the nurse's station, just down the hall."

By the time the doctor arrived, Mrs. Riddell had come to and was asking the same questions as Hodgins.

"I'm afraid he'll have to stay here a while." The doctor addressed Hodgins, occasionally glancing at Tom's mother. "He's taken quite a beating. It will be at least a week before we can properly assess that eye."

Mrs. Riddell gasped. "He won't be blind, will he?"

"I'm afraid it's too soon to say. Won't be able to examine it properly until the swelling goes down." The doctor turned his attention to Hodgins. "He has several broken ribs and his left ankle has a severe fracture. Almost broke right through, but not quite. Pretty much hanging by a thread, so to speak. That will take a long time to heal. We also suspect he has some internal bleeding as well. He's lucky to be alive."

Mrs. Riddell slumped in the chair.

"When she comes to, take her home, Henry. I'll let the boys at the station know how he is. I'm certain they'll all be out in full force to find who did this."

"What are you going to be doing, sir?"

"First, I'm going to check on Mrs. Robinson and Miss Shore. Then I'll try to find out who did this and why."

Hodgins went back to the station house briefly to let everyone know how Riddell was doing, then he headed north to The Junction, taking Harrington with him.

"Why are we going up there, detective? Not much that far north except the Carleton Race Course."

CHAPTER TWELVE

Hodgins flagged down the driver of a hack after he deposited his passenger across the road. "The Carleton Race Track, please."

Hodgins moved the blanket as it wasn't cold enough to need to cover their legs, and they settled in. "Gambling. Riddell was up there asking questions and now he's laying unconscious in the hospital. Coincidence? Maybe, maybe not. Someone knows something and I intend to find out what. If you haven't already guessed, you're my backup. I'm madder than a riled up hornet, but not foolish enough to go up there on my own. I've signed out a pistol, but I hope it's not going to be necessary."

Harrington gulped. "Them's a bad lot, I hear."

"You hear correctly, son."

They rode the rest of the way without speaking further. The driver let them off on Pacific Avenue and spun his cab around, racing his horses back into the city. Hodgins and Harrington walked until they came to the entrance. There were no races, but the gate wasn't locked, so they went in.

"Hey, you lot."

Hodgins turned towards the voice.

"Ain't open. Get lost."

Hodgins opened his coat and showed his badge. "Just looking for some information."

"Don't know nothin'." He waddled away, ripples of fat jiggling under his shirt.

"Wait, we aren't here to cause any trouble or make any arrests. I'm just trying to find out if one of my constables was here last evening. Tom Riddell." Hodgins gave a description of the young constable.

The employee shrugged.

"What's your name?"

"Everyone just calls me Fast Eddie."

Harrington snickered. Hodgins elbowed him.

"Eddie, I just need to know if Riddell was here yesterday. I'm investigating a murder and one of my suspects was thrown out of one of the gambling houses for cheating. Trying to find out which one.

"Yeah, young kid. Tossed out of the house a few blocks north. Don't know his name." Fast Eddie threw his head back and snorted.

Hodgins took the snort to be a laugh. "Yes, that would be Thomms. So, was my constable here looking for him?"

"Maybe. Wasn't here last night." His head turned at the sound of voices down the hall. "Gotta go. Said too much." Eddie shuffled off quicker than expected.

"Wonder what he's afraid of?" Harrington asked.

"More likely who, not what. Shall we see who's coming?" Hodgins walked towards the voices, Harrington close behind.

Two men rounded the corner just as Hodgins approached it. They all stopped, barely avoiding a collision. The men wore expensive suits and homburg hats. The tall one sneered.

"Coppers. I can smell 'em a mile away. Get lost." He walked past, purposely knocking shoulders with Hodgins.

"Not here to make trouble, just trying to trace one of my men's footsteps last night."

"Ya, he were here. Still trying to get the stench out." Both men broke out laughing.

Harrington took a step forward, but Hodgins held his arm out to stop him. "Funny. How long was he here?"

The tall one looked at the other man. "How long was he here, Knuckles? Didn't you escort him out?" Stretch emphasized *escort*.

"Ya, I escorted him." Knuckles made a fist and smacked it into his other palm. "I escorted him real good." He continued to punch his hand. "Ya want I should escort these two?"

"No." Stretch looked at Hodgins. "I believe they were just about to leave."

Hodgins and Harrington made a hasty retreat, not stopping until they were a block away.

"Why didn't we arrest him?" Harrington leaned against a tree, trying to catch his breath.

"No evidence. Can't arrest a man because he made a fist. At least we know Tom was here, and Thomms gambled at a house near the track. My guess is, it's run by Stretch back there. Young Thomms is lucky he didn't get the same treatment as Riddell."

"I doubt Thomms would've been able to take a beating as long as Riddell. Those students are soft. Couple of whacks from Knuckles would probably have killed him. Can't collect debts from a corpse."

"I wonder if William Keele knows what's going on at his track? Probably not. From what I know about him, he wouldn't put up with it. I'll have to make an appointment with him and let him know. Not going to be easy to rid the place of that kind of vermin. When we get back, see what you can find out about Knuckles. See if you can discover Stretch's name. Maybe I can plant a man at the track."

Harrington shook his head. "You heard him. He can smell a copper a mile away. Maybe a snitch?"

"No, not a snitch. But you've given me an idea. People like that are always looking for runners. I know one or two of the street urchins who don't mind helping, for a penny or two. They won't snitch for us, but I have used them a couple of times. They're very good at listening for information, and they can run fast. Part of the invisible people in the city. Citizens only see them to avoid them."

No cabbie willingly brought their horses so far north, so Hodgins and Harrington walked into the city. They waited for one of the horse-drawn trolleys to take them closer to the station, then walked the rest of the way. The officers stopped briefly at a street vendor for a mince pie.

When they arrived back, Harrington went in search of Knuckles' identity. Hodgins tossed some wood in the stove and warmed the kettle, trying to think of a way to convict Knuckles of assaulting Riddell. He jumped when someone spoke beside him.

"Barnes. Did you get Mrs. Harrington home? How is she?"

"Got her settled at the neighbour's so she wouldn't be alone. Her husband is at work and the rest of the children are in school. The doctor gave her something for her nerves.

Laudanum, I think. Tom woke up briefly. Mumbled something about horses, then conked out again."

"Come into my office." Hodgins shut the door once Barnes entered.

"I believe the horses refer to the Carleton Race Track. Since Riddell went up to the Junction, I thought that was a good place to start. Looks like someone called Knuckles beat poor Tom. Don't think I can get any evidence to convict him of it, but hopefully, we can get him for something else. Maybe the gambling. Sentence won't be as long, but it's better than nothing."

"What about Mr. Tufford?"

Hodgins slapped his forehead. "Plumb forgot. May as well head up to his neighbourhood now."

Barnes' stomach rumbled.

"And we can stop along the way and get you some food. Mince pies up the street are extra good today."

They walked up to College Street and took the trolley west to Lumley, where they began knocking on doors. Between the two of them, they discovered Mr. Tufford was an architect at Langley, Langley, and Burke on King Street, and was out of town consulting on a project. Everyone they spoke to agreed about his temper. No one noticed any friends ever paying him a visit, and Mr. Tufford declined any invitation to dine at the neighbours'. A very anti-social and unlikable chap. Despite his temper, not one neighbour could say they'd ever seen him strike a person, regardless of how agitated he became.

They made their way to the architectural firm and spoke with the partners and employees. The only new information they uncovered was his schedule. Tufford was to return home in two days.

Once back at the station, Hodgins sent Barnes to help Harrington with the search for the identities of the men at the race track. While he waited, he tore a clean sheet of foolscap off the pad on the desk and began a list.

- *Olive Robinson - deceased*

- *Mrs. Flora Robinson - hospitalized*

- *Mr. Jacob Robinson - deceased*

- *Miss Catherine Shore - hospitalized*

- *Barnabas (Barney) Robinson - survivor*

- *Bartholomew (Bart) Robinson - survivor*

- *Bennett (Benny) Robinson - survivor*

- *Susie Robinson - survivor*

- *Samuel Wright - deceased*

- *Lockerby, Adams, "Stubby" Gerrard, Simmons, and Thomms - students, friends of deceased*

- *George Franklin - childhood friend, matches description of person seen near murders*

Hodgins thought a moment, then added two more names and possible motives.

- *Knuckles - gambling*
- *Stretch - gambling*
- *Love letters - lovers spat? Spurned lover?*
- *Gambling debts and cheating*

He got up and went to his office door, looking around the station house for Barnes or Harrington.

One of the other constables noticed him and spoke up. "Sir, if you're looking for Henry and Floyd, I saw them go into the interview room with an armful of files."

"Hopefully, they find something. Thank you." He went back to his desk and stared at his list, unable to think of anything else to add to it. He paced around his office, muttering to himself.

"Why would anyone harm an entire family? How does the gambling fit in? Is it even relevant? Where the blazes is Franklin?"

Frustrated, he kicked the chair, knocking it over. "Damnation." He righted the chair and headed out, stopping at the sergeant's desk. "Back in an hour. Need to clear my head."

He wandered the streets, not paying any attention to where he went. Eventually, he ended up at the Toronto

General Hospital on Gerrard Street, north of Station Four. He went up to Riddell's room to check on the lad.

Riddell lifted his head slightly. "Sir?" It came out barely a whisper.

"Don't strain yourself. Just wanted to see how you're doing. You took quite a beating. I believe I know who did this, but it will be hard to prove. Your word against his. Got Barnes and Harrington looking for something. Anything. Nod your head if it was a thug that goes by Knuckles that did this."

Riddell nodded.

"Good. If we can't get him for this, I'll try for illegal gambling. That will get him off the streets for a little while, at least. Did you see a very tall man at the track?"

A slight nod.

"Did you hear his name?"

A shake.

A gasp at the doorway made Hodgins turn. Mrs. Riddell stood there with a man and two teen-aged children.

"Mrs. Riddell, come in." Hodgins stood and offered her the chair. "And this must be the rest of the family. I'm Detective Hodgins, and I promise we'll find the person who did this. Now, if you'll excuse me, I'll leave you to visit."

As Hodgins walked down the hall, Mrs. Riddell's sobs followed him. He headed west on Gerrard to the Allan

Horticultural Gardens, entered the wooden pavilion, and sat on one of the empty concert chairs.

This was the first time one of his men had been so severely attacked. Injury was always a risk, and occasionally death, but it was never easy to deal with. He'd seen several injuries as he rose through the ranks, along with death, but never since he'd become a detective. Most of his constables were young. They had decades ahead of them to marry, raise a family. A beating and possibility of partial blindness and permanent physical disability in their twenties was not something their families should be dealing with.

The wind picked up. The wooden structure rattled. Hodgins checked the time. Barnes and Harrington should've found something by now. He raised his collar and made his way back to the station.

The two constables were waiting for him.

"I think we found something." Barnes handed Hodgins a file. "Knuckles is actually Herman Duggan. One of his associates is Archibald Plunkett. Says he's six foot three. That sounds like Stretch."

Harrington gave Hodgins a second file. "Duggan has a rap sheet that would fill an entire cabinet. Mostly theft and assault. Plunkett has been arrested, but never charged. He's avoided any jail time. I think he has someone covering for him. The same person made most of the arrests. Sergeant

Moynehan. He's at Station Two now, but spent most of his time at One."

Hodgins skimmed both files. "Moynehan, eh? I've heard his name before. Rumour is they transferred him to clean up Station One's reputation. His grandfather was a cop. Fired along with the rest of the police force when the mayor cleaned up the graft and corruption back in the late 1850s."

"So it runs in the family," Barnes said. "Maybe we can get him along with Duggan and Plunkett."

Hodgins whistled. "Hard to take down a cop. Not good for your reputation either. You'd be labeled worse than a snitch." He thought for a minute. "But, if someone caught him in the act…"

"What do you have in mind, sir?" Harrington asked.

"I was thinking of that street urchin at the corner of King and Bay. Can't recall his name. About twelve, sandy hair, scar by his left eye."

"Oh, you mean Backstreet Billy."

"Yes, Billy. I need someone to ask for a job as a runner with Stretch Plunkett. Thought Billy would be a good one. He's fast, well known on the street. He's not a snitch, and that's something the bosses look for. I'll head over in a few minutes to look for him. Let me fill you in on my plan first."

CHAPTER THIRTEEN

Even though still fall, winter decided to arrive early. The temperature dropped several degrees overnight, so Hodgins decided against walking. He turned up his collar and tightened his scarf as he headed to the corner to look for a cabriolet or buggy. He flagged down the first one that came along and headed downtown to find Billy.

The wind picked up by the time he exited the cab. The horse's breath sent plums of white mist around its head, but it didn't seem to mind. It stomped its feet, eager to continue moving.

Hodgins walked up Bay Street, looking in the alleys as he passed. Some had children of varying ages huddled together. He asked them if they'd seen Billy, then rewarded them with a few pennies for food. They all said they didn't know him, but Hodgins suspected most lied. He didn't blame them. Most of the police gave the urchins a hard time.

Sometimes in the winter, on particularly bad days, a cop on the beat would take pity and arrest them, so they had a warm place for the night. Usually the older cops with small children. Unfortunately, most of the force chased them away and put out any fires they'd lit to keep warm.

He turned back and walked along King Street, repeating his pattern of asking and handing out coins. At the next corner, he spotted a newsboy acquainted with Billy.

"Whatcha lookin' fer Bill fer? He ain't done nothing."

"I know he hasn't done anything. I have a job for him. Bill knows me. Detective Hodgins."

The newsboy squinted at Hodgins. "Yeah. I heard Bill mention ya a time or two. Says yer all right, for a copper. I'll tell him.

Hodgins went back to the station to wait. Bill would likely send someone to the station with a message. He told the desk sergeant to expect one of the street kids and to make sure he didn't scamper off before Hodgins could speak with him. Most of them repeated the message and took off. He wanted to reward him, so he let Sergeant Cooper know.

The detective spotted a copy of *The Globe* on one of the desks and took it to his office while he waited. He read the article on the front page about the gale storm that raged Thursday evening and into Friday. Over seventy-five wrecks, including a ship on Lake Michigan, where twenty-two lost their lives, and the Schooner Emma on Lake Erie. Captain Scott not only lost his life, but that of his two daughters and nineteen others. Hodgins couldn't imagine how he'd react if he lost Sara, Holly, and Ivy. Even though they'd adopted the twins, they were just as much his family as if they were his own flesh and blood.

He flipped through, looking for any update on the petition one grocer started. He'd collected over five hundred signatures from other grocers, trying to get the city to ban costermongers. Someone had written a letter to the editor, taking the side of the peddlers. Why should people pay twenty-five cents for a peck of apples from the grocer when the peddler sold them for fifteen cents? The vendors wouldn't sell them if he couldn't make a profit, so the grocers must be making a pretty penny.

Hodgins hoped it didn't cause a problem. They didn't need a riot in the streets. He got halfway through the paper when a scuffle out front drew his attention. He went to his door and saw the sergeant trying to hang on to a child. The child broke free and ran out the door.

The sergeant turned to Hodgins. "Sorry, sir. I tried to stop her. I managed to slip a few pennies in her pocket, though. Said to meet Billy at John Mitchell's livery on Duke Street, soon as the sun goes down."

"Thank you." Hodgins pulled a few pennies from his pocket and handed them to the sergeant. "Slippery little thing, wasn't she?"

"Nothing but skin and bones. Afraid I'd break her if I held too hard." The sergeant looked at the money Hodgins gave him. "This is too much. Only gave her three pennies." He pocketed three and handed the rest of the coins to Hodgins.

"Keep them. Consider it payment for putting on a good show."

"Thank you." The sergeant's face turned a slight shade of pink as he turned away.

Before Barnes and Harrington left for home, Hodgins told them to be in his office first thing in the morning. He hoped he'd have an update from Billy by then.

As the sun went down, Hodgins walked to the stables. He figured Billy would've gone in earlier to hide. The temperature remained cold, but the snow had stopped midday. There's always someone around who might notice Billy going in shortly after a copper. Not good for his street reputation.

Hodgins walked in, nodding to the stable master. "Nice lot of horses you have here, Caleb. Might need to rent one later."

The stable master forked some hay into one of the stalls. "Nice pony three down. Tame enough for your daughter to handle."

Hodgins walked down to the pony and stroked her nose. Billy popped out from behind her. "Hear ya got a job fer me."

"I do, but it could be dangerous."

"Bah, I kin take care of m'self. What's the deal?"

"I'd like you to get a job as a runner for Plunkett. Rumour has it he's been running some sort of gambling den from the race track. Think you can handle it?"

Billy thought for a moment. "Tain't no rumour. Got some mean men working with him. He's always lookin' for fast boys. I kin do it."

Hodgins thought back to his encounter with Stretch Plunkett and Knuckles Duggan and what they'd done to Riddell. He'd never forgive himself if anything happened to the boy. "Maybe this wasn't such a good idea."

"I kin handle it. Whatchya need doing?"

"As I said, get a job as a runner. I need to know when and where he's setting up one of his gambling dens next. Knuckles put one of my constables in the hospital and I plan to bust him. He needs locking up. Can you do that? I'd need to know as soon as you find out."

"Easy. I've been a runner afore for the bookies. Everyone knows I'm fast and don't steal from them. Want I should go now?"

"The sooner the better. It's a long way up in the cold." He pressed some coins into Billy's hand. "Take a cab as close as you dare. Let me know what you find out. Can you meet me here in the morning?"

"I'll send word." Billy scampered out the back entrance.

Hodgins fed an apple to the pony, giving Billy time to get away. "Nice looking pony, Caleb. Maybe I'll let Sara take the reins when we go out for our Christmas tree."

When Hodgins got home, a rented carriage sat in front of his house. His in-laws had brought the children and dog back. Much as he'd enjoyed a few days alone with his wife, he longed for the noise. When he opened the door, Scraps ran down the hall and leapt up, pinning Hodgins against the door.

"I've missed you too, boy." Hodgins rubbed the dog's head, gently tugging his ears. "Now let me get my coat off." He took the dog's paws and guided Scraps down to the floor.

Scraps jumped and barked, running around in circles. As Hodgins tried to follow the sounds of voices down the hall, Scraps wound around his legs, almost tripping him, making the walk to the kitchen take twice as long as normal. His in-laws sat at the table, each with a toddler on their lap. Sara helped Cordelia cut vegetables for their dinner.

"Good evening, Euphemia, George. Enjoy your time with the children?"

"Immensely." George bounced Ivy on his knee, causing a round of giggles. "Glad to return them, though. Never been so tired in my life. Good tired."

"I understand completely. Enjoyed having Delia all to myself, but the house was too quiet."

Euphemia wrinkled her nose. "Next time we are not taking that beast."

Sara put her hands on her hips. "Grandmama, Scraps is not a beast."

CHAPTER FOURTEEN

Billy took the cabriolet north towards The Junction, jumping off several blocks short. He knew if anyone saw him arriving in a hansom, it would arouse suspicion. Street urchins never had money for such luxuries. Rather than walking straight into the track, he snuck in, making certain to be caught.

"Git yer hands off me. I were just lookin' for work. I'm a fast runner, I am. Ask anyone. Backstreet Billy's me name."

"Scrawny thing, ain't ya? Ya know what we do to people sneaking in?"

"Tol' ya. Lookin' for work. Ain't sneaking nowhere. Got anythin' I kin do?"

The man held tight to Billy's ragged coat tails, ready to toss him out, uncertain what to do. "Well, we lost a couple of boys last week. Buggers got caught pilfering."

"I ain't never been to jail. You kin trust me."

The man laughed. "Who said anything about jail? Couple of gutter rats like yurself. No one's gonna miss 'em." He thought for a moment, looking Billy over. "You might do. Skinny enough to fit through small spaces. If yur fast, boss might take ya on."

He shoved Billy along the dirt path. "This way."

They walked in a dimly lit area towards a back entrance. A lantern hung on a hook outside the door, the wick turned down so it cast little light. The man grabbed the wrought-iron handle and pulled the door open.

"In there." He shoved Billy hard enough to make him stumble.

Lanterns hung on the walls, flames turned down like the one outside the door. The floor sloped slightly. They rounded a corner and went down a staircase carved into the ground.

"Where ya takin' me? Thought you were gonna take me to the boss."

A short distance from the bottom of the stairs sat another door. The man opened it and shoved Billy in. "Wait here."

He picked up a plank resting against the wall and slid it into two wooden pieces placed on either side of the door to secure it.

They'd gone down deeper than most cellars. Darkness surrounded him, as there was nowhere any light could creep in. Billy banged his fists against the door. "Let me out."

His cries went unanswered. He walked around the room, hands searching the walls as he went. When he touched the door, he knew he'd gone all the way around. He'd come across no lanterns or torches. Even if he'd found one, he had no way to light it. He slid down the wall and leaned against it near the door, drawing his knees up and hugging them to try to keep warm.

CHAPTER FIFTEEN

Hodgins bid goodnight to his in-laws, who left shortly after the evening meal. Even though they adored their grandchildren, they were eager to return home to their quiet life. It pleased Cordelia that her parents accepted the twins they'd adopted earlier in the year. The girls' father was dead and their mother in jail.

Initially, Delia's mother, Euphemia, tried to talk them out of it, certain that the children would grow up to be no better than their parents. After spending time with them, she soon changed her mind. Hodgins never thought for a moment they'd have any issue with the girls, as they were only two when they took them in. He'd been told who took in the baby their mother had while in jail, but hadn't mentioned it to Cordelia yet. Eventually, they'd have to tell the girls about their natural parents, and that they had a little brother, but not for many years.

Once the children were all tucked in for the night, Hodgins and Cordelia sat in the front room by the fireplace, enjoying a cup of tea.

"I don't believe Mother will take the children again for some time. Did you see how tired she looked?" Cordelia set her cup down and picked up her embroidery.

"Can't say I noticed. You father was looking rather pale, though. He's not ill, is he?"

"Probably just worn out. Now, tell me everything you've learned about this horrid murder."

Hodgins laughed. "Are you planning on solving it for me? I could use some of your common sense. I believe it may involve gambling, but I can't for the life of me figure out how to connect it with the murders. Might be totally unrelated. One of the boys at the university, a childhood friend of Olive and Sam, seems to have a little gambling problem. Why that would make him murder any of the Robinsons is beyond me."

Delia placed her embroidery on her lap. "Well, maybe Mr. Robinson found out and was going to tell the boy's father. That would cause a scandal."

Hodgins nodded. "Yes, that's possible. But why murder or harm the rest of the family? Mr. Robinson was found in his work shed outside the house. The person could easily have killed him and left unseen. Instead, he went inside and bludgeoned Mrs. Robinson and her sister, and killed Olive. No. That just doesn't fit."

"Yes, I see what you mean. Didn't you mention a baby that wasn't home?"

Hodgins picked up his tea, nodding. "Susie." He drank the contents and sat the cup on the side table. "Mrs. Robinson's mother has her. Can't imagine what she'll tell her when she grows up."

"A much worse situation than we have with Holly and Ivy. How are the two ladies that are in the hospital?"

"Both are still in a coma. Doctors can't say if they'll survive. They have serious head wounds."

They both sat quietly for a moment, thinking about Sara and the twins. Cordelia picked up her embroidery, but just stared at it. She jumped when her husband spoke.

"I may have someone on the inside of one of the gambling dens up in The Junction. Hopefully he'll turn up something of use. Might even be able to connect an officer from one of the other stations to graft. They tossed his grandfather off the force a few decades ago, and the grandson has a bad reputation. Even if we can't connect the lad's gambling problem to the murders, maybe we can get a crooked cop off the force."

"And what of the red-headed man? Have you figured out who he is yet?"

Hodgins sighed. "No. Still haven't caught up with that lad in Newmarket. He's the only one who fits the description, but it seems like he might not be our man. Assuming, of course, what people up there have told me is true. I need to speak with him myself. His mannerisms may tell me a lot more than his words."

"Maybe it was someone in disguise. You know, wearing a wig and false sideburns."

"Hmm. That's something to look into. Anyone can purchase a wig, but where would one buy sideburns? Men don't generally go in for that sort of thing."

Cordelia resumed her stitching. "Why not ask around at the opera houses? They must purchase all sorts of things for their productions."

"Marvelous idea. I knew I married you for a reason." He smiled and stood. "Would you like more tea, dear?"

* * *

Next morning Hodgins hurried off to the station, eager to look into disguises. He stopped at Barnes' desk before bothering to take off his overcoat. "Henry, care to accompany me to the opera?"

Henry's eyebrows shot up. "The opera, sir? Wouldn't you rather take Mrs. Hodgins?"

Hodgins chuckled. "Not to see an opera, but now that you mention it, Delia might enjoy that. We discussed the case briefly last night and wondered if our red-haired man could be wearing a disguise. Delia suggested checking at the opera houses as they'd need costumes.

"You're lucky. Violet doesn't like to hear about my work. Especially if it's a murder. She's too delicate." Barnes stopped, his face turning red. "I don't mean to imply Mrs. Hodgins isn't delicate."

Hodgins waved a hand dismissively. "I know what you mean. Delicate is probably the last description I'd give of my wife. She's very much a lady, but she has a strong constitution and is quite curious. Delia loves a good puzzle. I expect Sara and the twins will follow her example."

"I wish Violet was a little more like her. Maybe after we've been married longer, she'll be less shocked at what we do. Are we going to the opera house now?"

"I doubt there will be many people there this early. Give it a few hours. Hopefully the costumers will be in. Why don't you check on Riddell? I have an appointment with Mr. Keele to let him know what's going on at his track. Meet me back here at ten."

CHAPTER SIXTEEN

After finding nothing of use at the Royal, Hodgins and Barnes continued to the Grand Opera House. They stood across the street, taking in the magnificent building. "What do you think, Barnes? Fancy enough?"

Barnes stared at the four-storey building. On top of the fourth floor sat a clock tower, centred perfectly above the arched entrance. "Spectacular. I wonder if Violet would like to attend a performance some time."

"If she's anything like Delia, she'll welcome the opportunity to dress up in her finest."

They crossed, careful to dodge the droppings left by the horses. Hodgins pulled at the main door and found it locked. "Must be a stage entrance around the side. Let's see what's down Johnson Lane."

They walked down the west side of the opera house and found a side door, unlocked. Hodgins opened it and they entered.

"Sorry, gentlemen, but we're not open yet." The man noticed Barnes' uniform. "Problem, officers?"

Hodgins showed his badge. "Detective Hodgins. No, there's no problem. We were hoping to speak with the costume designer."

"The head seamstress is in the dressing rooms. Down the hall on your right."

The first door they came across was ajar, so Hodgins knocked and walked in. "Hello?"

"If yer here ta tell me there's another change, I'll sew your lips together."

They followed the voice and found an elderly woman at a table, hidden behind a rack of costumes.

"No changes, ma'am, just questions." He introduced himself and Barnes. "Do you have a moment?"

"Sure, Sonny. My fingers could use a rest. Name's Charlotte."

Barnes pulled out his notebook, ready to make notes while Hodgins asked the questions. He kept his head down so Hodgins couldn't see him grinning at the detective being called Sonny.

"We're looking for a man that doesn't seem to exist. Thought maybe he wore a disguise and we aren't certain where he might get one. Since the players at the opera house wear costumes, we were hoping you might be able to help."

Charlotte nodded. "Yes, there are a few places to buy them. Probably have to have it custom made, though. What sort of disguise are you looking for?"

"Red-hair and mutton chops. Don't suppose anyone's been here asking you to make them?"

"Sorry, Sonny. Several places in the city to buy a wig. Red's not the most popular, but I'm sure he could get red-hair from a barber."

"Is it possible he could have stolen something from here? The side door is unlocked. Do you have any costumes requiring a red wig?"

She placed a finger at the side of her mouth while she thought. "Lady Macbeth is frequently portrayed with dark ginger hair. Should have that costume around somewhere. It's a lady's wig though. No sideburns."

"Pair of shears would take care of that. Cut off some hair and make the mutton chops with it. Can you check to see if it's still here?"

She slid off the stool and scurried to the far side of the room. The rummaging and moving of boxes and the sliding of hangers filled the room.

"It's not here." She came back empty-handed. "Got the costume, but the wig's missing. We haven't done Macbeth for almost a year. No reason anyone would need it."

Barnes scribbled in his notebook. "Might be the thief and murderer are the same person."

"Possibly." Hodgins turned to the seamstress. "Thank you for your time, Miss Charlotte."

As they left, Barnes hesitated.

"Something wrong, Henry?"

"Just wondering if I could peek into the theatre. Probably the only chance I'll get to see the insides of a place so grand."

"Don't suppose it would do any harm. There's a door over there."

Barnes opened the door and stepped in. "Sir, have you ever seen anything so magnificent? It certainly lives up to its name. How big do you think that stage is?"

A familiar voice answered. "It's fifty-three feet wide and sixty-five feet deep."

They turned to see the man they first encountered.

"Would you like a tour, officers?"

They both nodded.

"Let's go to the front and start there." He led them to the lobby and pointed at the arched entrance way. "Theatre-goers walk though there into our plush reception area. It's fifty feet deep. Next, the main foyer. People can purchase their tickets there, at the booth, or get refreshments at the bar at intermission. Those stairways lead up to the balconies." He opened the doors to the main theatre. "We can accommodate over thirteen hundred patrons."

Hodgins extended a hand to their guide. "I'm happy to say I've had the pleasure of being one of those thirteen hundred. Thank you for the tour, Mr.?"

"Langston, sir."

"Thank you, Mr. Langston." Hodgins shook his hand.

"Yes, thank you." Barnes turned in a circle, taking in all the gas lamps. "Maybe one day I can bring my wife here."

"Was Miss Charlotte of assistance?"

"Yes, most helpful. Good day, sir." Hodgins glanced at Barnes' expression. *Now I know what to get him for Christmas.*

Hodgins and Barnes walked over to Yonge Street and headed north.

"It's too bad the wig was stolen. Much easier to find the killer if he'd asked to have it and the sideburns made." Barnes kicked a pebble on the walkway.

"Agreed. At least it more or less confirms the thought the killer wore a disguise. I wonder if he knows his way around the theatre? Miss Charlotte didn't mention a mess being made. Could he have known exactly where to find the red wig? Or was it just happenstance the first one he found was red?"

Barnes mulled it over for a moment. "I think he knew. Miss Charlotte said they hadn't used it for ages. Wouldn't there be other wigs closer to the door he could have grabbed?"

"Good point. So, we need to decide if he thought ahead and went for something that wouldn't be missed any time soon, or maybe heard someone coming and hid, then took what was at hand. When we get back, make a list of the barbers and see if anyone's been asking for red clippings."

"Sir! Do you know how many barbers are in the city?"

"A lot. Get Harrington to split the list with you."

CHAPTER SEVENTEEN

Billy scrambled to his feet when the door opened. A little light shone in from the lanterns in the passageway. He recognized the man. "Yer the one they called Knuckles, ain't ya?"

"Smart kid. Follow me. Boss wants ta see ya."

Knuckles led him back outside and into one of the racetrack offices. Stretch Plunkett sat behind a large oak desk.

"Welcome to my team, Billy. I had my men ask around about you. Word is you're fast and reliable. Just what I'm looking for. Come back tonight at ten o'clock. My friend here will take to you tonight's game. Off with you now. Remember, ten sharp."

Billy raced out, not stopping for several blocks. He reached into his pocket, his fingers curling around the rest of the money Hodgins had given him. He noticed a driver dropping off a passenger down the street and almost flagged him down. The rumble in his stomach stopped Billy from waving his hand. Instead, he continued south, deeper into the city, where he knew he'd find a street vendor.

After filling his belly, he gave a penny to one of the smaller street kids to run to the station to tell Hodgins they'd given him the job.

CHAPTER EIGHTEEN

odgins skimmed the newspaper, trying to fill time before heading to Union Station to take the train back to Newmarket. The next one didn't leave for a few hours and they had no new leads to follow up on. He looked up when someone knocked on his door. Sergeant Cooper stood in the doorway, hand tightly clasp to a little girl's shoulder.

"Message from Billy, sir. Made certain this one didn't skedaddle off."

Hodgins came around his desk and knelt in front of her so his height didn't intimidate her. "What's your name, honey?"

The girl wiggled, trying to dislodge the hand holding her.

"I'm not going to hurt you. I have three daughters. Sara, Holly, and Ivy."

She narrowed her eyes, staring at him suspiciously.

"Fine. What's the message?"

"Billy got the job. Can I go now, mister?"

"Good." Hodgins stood and pulled some coins from his pocket. "Here. Take her to the vendor on the corner and get her a hot pie. Give her the change."

The sergeant took the money. "Very generous of you, sir." He looked down at the thin shawl around the girl's shoulder. "My Betsy outgrew her coat. Can you come back tomorrow, sweetheart? Get a nice warm coat."

She looked at the sergeant, then at Hodgins, and stopped struggling. "Maybe."

Cooper led her out, but she stopped and turned towards Hodgins. "Thanks, mister."

Hodgins went over to Barnes' desk and sat on the corner. "Any news on Riddell?"

"Might be able to go home in a week or so, but the doctor said he probably won't be back to work until after the new year, assuming he'll mend properly at all."

"Let's hope the injuries heal. Don't know what he'll do if he can't be a copper. His job will be here when he's well."

"Tom will be happy to hear that. I'm going to stop in on my way home. I got the new Jules Verne book. He should like that. I know he liked the others, especially *20,000 Leagues Under the Sea.*"

"Yes, he seems to like those adventure books quite a bit. I'll visit him again soon." Hodgins sighed. "Just found out young Billy got a job with Plunkett. I hope he doesn't end up like Riddell."

Neither spoke for a few minutes, then Hodgins tapped the newspaper sitting on the desk. "Just reading about the new courthouse and Station One construction. They expect to be done by early December."

"A new building? Guess it won't be as drafty as this one."

"Thinking of asking for a transfer?" Hodgins grinned at the look on Barnes' face.

"No, sir. I'd never—Oh, you're joshing me. Good one. Wouldn't mind having a wander through it once it opens, though."

Hodgins turned when he heard whistling. Cooper had returned. "Why so happy, Cooper?"

"Just feel good. Once Sal got food in her belly, she turned into quite the chatterbox."

"Sal? So she finally gave up her name."

"She's been alone on the streets for about a year. Both parents died when their house caught fire and she has no other family. Been dodging the authorities all this time."

Hodgins grinned. "If I know you, you'll be talking to your wife about her tonight."

"Betsy's mentioned she wished she had a little sister. How's your Sara taken to have two little ones in your home?"

"Wonderfully. It was her idea, after all. And it feels good giving a home to someone in need."

Cooper nodded, then continued whistling as he made his way back to his desk.

"That's real nice of him. Give the little mite an early Christmas. I know Violet wants several children." Barnes leaned back in his chair. "Two or three would be nice."

"Wait until after the first and see if you don't change your mind." Hodgins laughed, then checked the time. "Train for Newmarket leaves in just under an hour. Best get a move on. Franklin should have returned home by now.

* * *

Hodgins stepped off the train, grabbing his hat when a chilly gust of wind came out of nowhere. He chuckled as he watched one gentleman rush down the platform, chasing a homburg. Several ladies stood against the ticket booth, a tight grip on their dress skirts, waiting for the wind to die down.

On the ride up, Hodgins' mind had flipped back and forth, trying to decide whether to go to Franklin's home or place of employment. Not wanting to deal with Mrs.

Franklin again, or her neighbour, he'd opted for the Borland. Besides, it was closer to the train station.

Fifteen minutes later, he ordered a pot of tea and sat at a corner table with the mysterious George Franklin.

"Mother said you were looking for me. She told me about Olive and her family. I'd like to attend the service."

"I can make certain word is sent. The bodies should be released soon." Hodgins opened his notebook and flipped through his notes.

"One of their neighbours said she spoke to a red-haired man, around Olive's age, shortly before the murders. Another saw a young man peeping in a window around the same time."

Franklin shook his head. "On my honour, I have not been to Newmarket for quite some time."

Hodgins turned to a clean page and made a few notes. "When was the last time you sported mutton chops?"

Franklin laughed. "Mutton chops? I have never had sideburns of any sort. My red hair makes me stand out as it is. Mutton chop would be too much."

Hodgins pictured him with the bushy sideburns and laughed. "Yes, I see what you mean. One more question. Have you ever gone by the nickname Frankie?"

"No. Well, not recently. Why do you ask?"

"We found some old love letters signed Frankie in Olive's room."

Franklin turned almost as red as his hair. "She kept them? Surprising, as she did not return my affections. And before you ask, I harboured no ill will towards her. We remained friends until I moved. Our old chums will confirm that."

Hodgins jotted in his book again. "Did Sam Wright know about your feelings towards his fiancé?"

"I don't know. If he found out, it wasn't from me. I must send my condolences."

Hodgins put down his pencil. "I'm sorry to tell you, but Mr. Wright has also been murdered."

"Dear Lord. Please don't tell me his family was harmed as well?"

"No, just him. I'll need to know where you've been the past week."

"Yes, of course." Franklin provided the name and address of who he had visited, then called to the bartender for a shot of whisky. He downed it in one gulp.

"Is there anything else, Detective? I need to get back to work."

"No, that's all."

"Get you more tea?"

"No, a beer. Then I'll head back to the city."

CHAPTER NINETEEN

Hodgins walked Scraps while Cordelia cleared up after supper. When he returned, Scraps shook off the snow, ran to the kitchen, then flopped on his mat by the wood-burning stove. Hodgins retired to the sitting room. A few minutes later, Cordelia joined him, carrying two cups of tea.

"You look rather deflated, Bertie. Still no idea who harmed that poor family?"

Hodgins stood, taking both cups so Delia could settle on the chair opposite him. He handed her one cup, then added more wood to the fire with his free hand. He sighed and returned to his chair.

"That's the problem. I have too many ideas. Initially, I thought the lad in Newmarket could have done it. He's the only red-haired man we've found. But now?" He shrugged. "There's a very good possibility the killer wore a disguise. Could've been anyone."

Cordelia blew on her tea before taking a sip. "But which one has a motive?"

"That, my dear, is an excellent question. So far, we have a letter from an angry customer and love letters from a rejected suitor. Both were out of town when the murders took place, but I'll have one of the constables follow-up to confirm their whereabouts. For one of them to have committed the murders, he would have been noticeably absent for quite some time. And I believe Sam Wright's murder is connected. It can't be a coincidence the fiancé met the same fate and a mysterious red-haired man was spotted once again, could it?"

Cordelia put her cup on one of the small, round side tables and retrieved her knitting. "It must be a crime of passion, but why harm anyone other than Olive?"

"Precisely. If it was a crime of passion, as you said, they would've killed only Olive and Sam. We're missing something. Maybe when I go in tomorrow Barnes will tell me he found the man wearing the disguise."

* * *

Barnes knocked on Hodgins' office door the next day and walked in. "Afraid I'm having no luck with the barbershops, sir. Harrington's completed his list, and I've been to most of those on mine. No one's had anyone requesting red hair. Most said they don't even have any ginger customers. I'll keep asking once they open for the day."

"Maybe you'll get lucky. Something's bound to turn up, eventually. I just hope it's not another body."

Shortly after Barnes left, Dr. Stonehouse came in. Hodgins wondered how he'd managed to stay single, what with him being both good-looking and a doctor. The mother of every unmarried daughter probably kept his social calendar full with dinner and party invitations. Hodgins motioned to the chair, inviting the coroner to sit.

"Just wanted to let you know the bodies of Mr. Robinson and his daughter have been released. Mrs. Shore asked to have them sent to the undertaker. Murphy and Company on Yonge Street. They'll be interred at the Duchess Street Burying Ground."

Hodgins searched his memory for a moment. "Duchess? Isn't that run by the Knox Presbyterian?"

Stonehouse settled in the chair opposite Hodgins and crossed his legs. "Yes. Since Mrs. Shore was still quite upset, she asked me to speak to the minister, Alexander Topps. With her being a widow, I don't know how she's going to pay. They'll probably end up in pauper graves."

Hodgins leaned back. "That's a shame. Two proper burials would be a little pricey. Maybe as much as a hundred dollars, I imagine."

Stonehouse nodded but made no attempt to leave.

Hodgins smiled. "Once we catch the killer, you'll have to join my wife and me for a meal. Of course, she'll invite one of her friends. She already has a few in mind who might suit you. Most of her friends are quite open-minded and don't object to talk of murder and death. I believe she's recently made the acquaintance of a medium. Don't believe in that myself, but I'm willing to be proven wrong."

The doctor stood. "A medium, eh? That would make for a lively discussion, if you'll excuse the pun."

"I'll mention that to my wife. Maybe we'll get a demonstration."

They shook hands, and the doctor returned to the morgue. Hodgins leaned back, tipping his chair onto the rear legs, thinking about Cordelia's psychic friend. A knock on the door jolted him, causing the chair to tip back further. Fortunately, the chair was close enough to the wall to prevent an embarrassing accident.

Barnes grinned. "Sorry, sir. Finished up with the barber shops. No luck. Guess that means the wig is our only clue."

"Yes, and not much of one. It narrows our suspect list down to every college-age young man in the city. Glad you popped in. I was having the most absurd thought. You can laugh if you want."

Barnes perched on the edge of the chair. "Never, sir."

"Stonehouse was here earlier. Cordelia is trying to trap the poor man into marriage with one of her friends. She's got this new acquaintance—a medium." He watched Barnes' expressions. Not even a hint of amusement.

"Maybe she can help, sir? My mother used to tell me tales of a great aunt who communicated with the other side. She died when I was just a sprig, but the stories were uncanny."

"So, you're a believer in such things?"

"Well, I don't *not* believe, exactly. And it wouldn't harm the case none."

Hodgins twisted the end of his mustache. "True. And as John Heywood wrote, *Nothing ventured, nothing gained.*"

"Who?"

"English writer. Maybe tonight I'll speak to my wife and see what she thinks. Her friend may not want to help. And Barnes, keep this to yourself, eh?"

"Mum's the word."

Sergeant Cooper knocked on Hodgins' office door. "Pardon the interruption, but one of those street urchins left word. Billy wants to meet you at the usual place."

"He must have information. When?"

"Right away, Detective."

"Thank you, Cooper."

Barnes stood when the sergeant left. "Usual place?"

"Livery." Hodgins reached for his overcoat. "Shouldn't be long."

* * *

Hodgins entered the livery and looked around. There was no sign of Billy.

"Chestnut bay."

Hodgins turned to see who spoke. "Who's there? Caleb? Is that you?"

A head appeared over the gate of a stall. "He's with the chestnut down at the end. When you gonna take those girls of yours out for a ride? Special rate goes up the longer your wait."

"Soon. I promise." Hodgins headed to the last stall to find his young accomplice.

Billy stood beside the large horse, brushing her side. Hodgins picked up another and brushed the other side.

"What have you got for me, Billy? Haven't heard from you for days."

"Bin keeping busy. They got me running money fer the horse racing. Bets made by Stretch's private customers. Tonight will be me first at the gambling house."

"Good. Keep your eyes and ears alert for anyone who looks college age, or anyone talking about young lads. I have a feeling Thomms will try to get back in. He owes quite a bit and will want to try to win so he can pay off his debt. If he's smart, he'll ask his father for the money and take his punishment. I'm certain it'll be much better than what Knuckles will give him."

"Count on me. Ain't seen little Sal for days. Kin ya find out what happened to her?"

"Not to worry. Sergeant Cooper and his wife took her in."

Billy's jaw dropped. "She's got a home? Honest?"

"Honest. She's not been on the street long, I understand."

"Nope. Glad to hear it. Street's no place for young'uns like her. Too soft. Haveta be born on the streets to survive. This Cooper fella. He's okay?"

"Yes. Has one daughter already, not much older than Sally. From what he told me, she's settled in already."

"Good. I'll try to send word tomorrow." Billy dropped the brush on top of a bale of hay and scooted out the back door.

CHAPTER TWENTY

During supper that evening, Hodgins asked Cordelia about her new friend. "Do you think she'd have any interest in meeting the new coroner?"

Cordelia put her fork down. "Funny you should mention that. We've already spoken about him. She's intrigued, but what would Doctor Stonehouse think about her being a medium?"

"What does her size matter, Mamma?" Sara looked at her mother. "Won't he like her if she's not skinny?"

Cordelia laughed. Hodgins almost spit out his tea.

"No, dear. Not her size. A medium. A spiritualist. Do you know what that is?"

Sara shook her head.

"It's someone who communicates with the dead. Only special people can do that. They're called mediums, or psychics."

"Or frauds and cons," Hodgins mumbled into his teacup.

Cordelia glared at him. "Hush."

Sara's eyes went wide. "Honest? How can anyone talk to a dead person?"

"I don't know. I don't think even they know themselves. Not everyone can do it, but there are plenty who pretend, just so they can take money from people who are terribly upset at the loss of a loved one."

"That's mean."

"Yes, dear. It's very mean. But my friend isn't like that."

"Can she come over and talk to a dead person for us?"

Hodgins joined the conversation. "Yes, Delia. Can she? I was going to suggest it myself. I'm desperate and thought it would be worth a try to see if she could contact one of the Robinson's. Like Barnes said, it won't hurt."

The corner of Cordelia's mouth twitched. "You've already discussed it? So, you believe she can speak with the dead? What about the doctor? What would he think?"

"Actually, I discussed it with him earlier today. He's interested. Told him I'd have him over for a meal when we solve the case."

"Why wait? I'll send a note to Amelia tomorrow and invite her to join me for lunch at one of the restaurants downtown. If she's agreeable to both the doctor and a demonstration, you can invite him to participate."

"Me too?"

Cordelia looked from Sara to her husband. He shrugged.

"We'll see. Now, finish your meal and help your sisters or you won't get any cake."

Once the children were finally in bed, Hodgins and Cordelia retired to the front parlour. Hodgins settled in the chair by the fire to read the paper, while Cordelia sat at the davenport desk.

"Catching up on your correspondence, Delia?"

"Inviting Amelia to luncheon. Would you mail it in the morning so she receives it in the first post? It's amazing how quickly correspondence is delivered. Wouldn't surprise me if in the future, mail is delivered almost as soon as one puts it in the box. And it's so nice to finally have help with the household and be able to meet friends at barely a moment's notice. Violet's friend Beryl gets along so well with the children, but I'm not sure how long we'll have her before she finds a beau and weds."

Hodgins looked over the top of the newspaper. "Hopefully, Violet has enough single friends to last until we don't need a nanny. Leave your mail in the pocket of my overcoat and I'll pop it in the post. And I hope your friend isn't strange. We've had a few of her type in the jail recently, and they've all been… peculiar."

Delia's back straightened, her tone sharpened. "I'll ask her to be normal, just this once."

* * *

Cordelia rushed to get ready to meet Amelia. She'd replied immediately that she was available and suggested meeting at The Senator on Victoria Street at one. While Cordelia changed, Beryl played with the twins before feeding them. "Beryl, can you help me, please? I can't get my dress fastened."

Beryl rushed across the hall to assist. "There, all buttoned up. Who are you lunching with?"

"A new acquaintance. When I return, I'll tell you all about her. Now, I really must rush. I should be home before Sara is out of school." Cordelia went into the twin's room and kissed them before leaving.

Twenty minutes later, she entered the restaurant. Cordelia looked for her friend and spotted a hand waving at a table near the back.

"I hope you haven't been waiting long, Amelia."

"Not at all. I was so glad to receive your invitation." Amelia's voice was soft, with a slight French accent.

"I must admit, I have an ulterior motive. A few, actually. Of course, I wanted to see you. We have such lively conversations. First, if you're still agreeable, it seems Doctor Stonehouse is interesting in making your acquaintance. Second, my husband was wondering if you would agree to try to contact one of his murder victims."

Amelia smiled. "The doctor, he knows of me, oui? And he is not, how you say? Put off?"

"Not at all. My husband said Doctor Stonehouse is very eager to meet you. Apparently, he's quite open-minded about your abilities. Would you be agreeable to coming to my home and doing a demonstration of sorts? Bertie wants to see first hand before he decided if he believes or not. He'll invite the doctor, too."

The waiter arrived, interrupting their conversation. Once they placed their orders, Amelia considered the request. "What sort of demonstration? You know I do not perform tricks."

"I'd never suggest such a thing. If you could contact someone he knows who has passed, then he couldn't call you a fraud. He's had several fake spiritualists in his jail recently, so he's a little skeptical. But he's willing to be convinced."

"Yes. I will demonstrate. Would tomorrow evening be convenient?"

"Perfect. I'll stop at the police station on the way home and tell him. I'll let him go to the coroner's office to invite the doctor."

"If I don't find your husband's reaction réprehensible, objectionable, I will consider helping him with his murder. Tell me, how long ago did this murder take place?"

"Murders actually. Two family members and a young man. About a week ago."

"The family in the newspaper? Terrible. Yes, I will help, regardless."

* * *

Cordelia asked the driver to wait while she went into the police station to speak with her husband. A light snow fell, so the driver put a blanket over the horse while he waited.

"Good afternoon, Sergeant Cooper. Is my husband available?"

"Yes, ma'am. He's in his office."

"Thank you." Cordelia made her way across the office. Hodgins' door stood open. "Ahem."

Hodgins looked up. "Delia! Is something wrong? Come in. Sit."

She waved him off. "Nothing is wrong. Just stopped on my way home to tell you Amelia will be coming over tomorrow evening. Make certain to invite Doctor Stonehouse. My carriage is waiting. Now, don't forget the doctor."

She turned to leave and almost walked into Constable Barnes. "Afternoon, Henry. You and Violet can come too." Cordelia hurried out without explaining.

Barnes went into Hodgins' office. "Sir?"

"Her spiritualist friend is coming over tomorrow evening. Not sure what to expect. Would you and Violet care to join us?"

"I would, but my wife wouldn't. She's afraid of such things. Besides, her folks are coming to dinner. Will this friend help with the murders?"

"Guess I'll find out tomorrow."

CHAPTER TWENTY-ONE

Hodgins got Dr. Stonehouse settled in the front parlour just as someone knocked on the front door. "Brace yourself, doctor. Your future wife may just have arrived." *Please don't let her be too strange.*

Cordelia stopped fussing with the dining room table and hurried to answer. Sara ran past and opened it.

"Bonne soirée, mon cher. You must be Sara."

"Yes, ma'am. Bonne soirée."

Cordelia stood behind Sara, hands resting on her shoulders. "Amelia. Thank you for coming. Let me take your coat. I've put a lovely lace cloth on the table, and two tall, white candles, as you requested. My husband and Doctor Stonehouse are in the parlour. Allow me to make introductions."

Both men stood when Cordelia and Amelia entered the room. "Amelia, I'd like you to meet my husband, Albert, and our friend, Doctor Stonehouse. This is my friend, Amelia Alarie."

Stonehouse took Amelia's hand and kissed it. "Enchanté. I'm looking forward to observing you at work. And please, call me Valentine."

Amelia smiled. "Valentine. A Latin name, non? Means strength and health. Fitting for a doctor."

Stonehouse laughed. "Considering I became a coroner, health might not be terribly appropriate."

"Are we going to start soon, Mama?"

"Sara! Manners."

"No, the child is correct. I came to provide a demonstration for your husband. Sara is open and inquisitive. She will have an exciting life."

Sara beamed and took Amelia's hand. "This way. Mama said she might let me light the candles."

As she passed the table, Amelia picked up one of the silver candlesticks, holding it in both hands for several seconds. After returning it to its place, she turned to Hodgins. "These were your mother's. She is present, watching over the children." She took the seat at the far end of the table and placed a set of tarot cards in front of her. "Sit."

Cordelia and Sara sat to her left. Hodgins and Stonehouse took the chairs to her right. Amelia nodded to Sara.

"Go ahead. But be careful." Cordelia handed her daughter the box of wooden matches. Sara lit the candles and returned to her chair.

"I require silence." Amelia closed her eyes, hands clasped primly on the tabletop. A breeze wound around the table. Sara gasped and rubbed her arms, as did Cordelia. Hodgins and Stonehouse exchanged a look.

The candles flickered. Amelia swayed slightly. Her lips moved, but no sound came out. She stopped suddenly, opening her eyes. She turned to the detective.

"Your mother is concerned for her other son. She wishes you to keep him safe from further harm."

Hodgins looked across the table at Cordelia. She shook her head. "I never mentioned Jonathan."

"It was in the newspapers." Hodgins crossed his arms and sat back.

Amelia smiled. "She asks if you have placed any more fish under your bed."

Cordelia giggled. "That wasn't in the newspaper."

"Still not convinced, but I'm intrigued. I'll speak with Jonathan and see what he's up to. He promised no more dodgy deals. What about the murdered family?"

"Your mother's presence is too strong. No one else is being allowed to come through. She is happy about the twins and how Sara is taking care of them."

Sara smiled and clapped her hands.

Hodgins leaned forward, placing his elbows on the table. "What if I allowed you into their home?"

"Oui, that would be most useful."

"Are we going to play cards now?" Sara pointed to the tarot deck.

"No, cher. These are special cards to tell your past, present, and future. Would you like to know your future, Sara?"

"Oh, yes, please."

"Come. Stand beside me." Amelia shuffled the deck, then handed the cards to Sara. "Cut them anywhere, then place the bottom half on top."

Sara did as instructed.

Amelia picked up the cut cards and cradled them in both hands, concentrating on her question for the child. "As you are still young, I will not do a past and present. Only what the future holds for your happiness, your path in life." She drew the top three cards and placed them face down on the table. She turned the first card over.

"The ten of Pentacles, upright. You will have success in your endeavours, an abundance of wealth, and possible fame.

Amelia turned over the next card. "The fool."

Sara giggled.

"The Fool is a traveller. This card is also upright."

"What does it mean when you say upright?" Sara looked up at Amelia.

"Upright is good, or positive. If the card is reversed, upside down, it has a different meaning. It would show recklessness. Would you like to see the last card?"

Sara nodded, eyes wide.

"The Star. Again, upright. All good signs. Faith, hope, purpose. You have a wonderful future."

"I'll travel and be rich."

"Yes, but wealth has many meanings, not just money. You are already wealthy. Family and friends are priceless."

"Time for bed, Sara. You can dream about travelling the world. Off with you." Cordelia stood and placed an arm around Sara's shoulder.

"Good night, Miss Amelia. Thank you for telling my future. Good night, Doctor Stonehouse." Sara kissed both parents and skipped upstairs.

"That was quite interesting. I am curious about the fish." Stonehouse turned in his chair to face Hodgins.

Hodgins sighed. "When I was a lad, my brother took me fishing. We were supposed to be at school. I was proud of the fish I caught, but afraid my parents would find out we were truant. I hid it under my bed. Well, it wasn't long before it began to rot. Stunk up the bedroom something fierce. Can still feel the paddling I got just thinking about it."

"What do you think about Amelia's gift now, Bertie?" Cordelia walked around the room, raising the wicks on the lanterns, then returned to the table to extinguish the candles.

"Must admit, I don't know how she knew about the fish. Won't say I'm thoroughly convinced, but it does make one pause. I rather like the idea Mother is keeping an eye on the children." Hodgins turned to their guest. "Amelia, would you be available tomorrow to visit the Robinson's home? I can even make certain the station compensates you for your time."

"You can expense a medium?" Stonehouse raised an eyebrow.

"A consultant. I don't need to specify. If asked, I'll just say it's a second opinion on the cause of death."

"Not sure if I should be insulted or not. I suppose, in a way, we are in the same field." Stonehouse stood. "I've had a most enjoyable evening, but I should head home. It was a pleasure to finally meet you, Mrs. Hodgins, and you as well, Miss Alarie."

"I should be leaving as well. Even a small demonstration leaves me a little drained."

"We'll have to have you both over again, for a meal, not a reading." Hodgins and Delia walked their guests to the door.

Stonehouse helped Amelia with her coat. "I drove over in my buggy. May I give you a lift?"

"Oui, merci." Amelia turned to Hodgins. "Tomorrow afternoon?"

Hodgins raised an eyebrow. "It doesn't need to be after dark?"

"No, the spirits will talk if they need resolution. Time no longer has meaning to them."

"Three o'clock, then? I'll get your address from Delia and pick you up. One of my constables will meet us there with the key. Barnes was most disappointed he couldn't attend tonight. This may make up for that."

CHAPTER TWENTY-TWO

Barnes stood waiting on the front steps of the Robinson home when Hodgins and Amelia pulled up to the curb. Hodgins tied the horse to a tree and assisted Amelia down.

Barnes came to the curb to greet them. "Rather large carriage, sir."

"Took the family to church in style. If the weather holds out, we'll go for a ride before the evening meal. Miss Alarie, this is Constable Barnes."

"Bonne journée, Constable."

"G'day, miss. I wish I could've attended last evening, but my in-laws were over for supper. I had a great aunt with the gift, but I never met her."

"This isn't a social call, Barnes. Shall we get started?"

"Sorry, sir." Barnes pulled the key from his pocket and unlocked the door.

As soon as Amelia crossed the threshold, she gasped. "There is death, yet not death, everywhere." She swayed.

"Are you all right?" Hodgins took her arm to steady her.

"Oui. So many souls. Two are in between, not yet crossed over."

"Well." Hodgins hesitated. "Two have been badly injured and are still at the hospital, unresponsive. Do you need to step out?"

"No. I am fine." Amelia hesitated at the doorway to the front parlour. "There are two spirits here, but in between." She pointed down the hall. "One attacked there, another in this room."

Amelia walked into the parlour. "Both are women. Sisters. Their spirits are together, confused." She left the room and stood at the foot of the stairs.

"You don't want to go up there, miss. It's quite, um, messy." Barnes stepped in front of Amelia.

"Yes, I feel it. So brutal—" She fainted, falling forward towards Barnes.

He fell backwards as Amelia made contact, his foot catching the bottom step. Hodgins rushed to grab Amelia, but couldn't reach her before she fell on Barnes, the two landing in a heap.

"Get her off me, sir. She's out cold and rather heavy for such a tiny woman."

Hodgins lifted Amelia's slight form off Barnes and carried her into the sitting room. Gently, he placed her on the settee, then turned to check on Barnes.

"I'm fine. Step bit into my back, but that's all. How's Miss Alarie?" Barnes reached around to rub the small of his back.

"Still out cold. I'll fetch a wet cloth from the kitchen." Hodgins grabbed the first towel he saw and pumped cold water onto it. He wrung it out and returned to Amelia, placing the folded towel on her forehead.

She moaned, then opened her eyes.

"I am sorry. So many speaking at once. This house has several old souls who need assistance. The ones recently murdered are not alone here. They knew the man who killed them. I will come another day if permitted as I need to prepare myself for the old ones. I will also try to help the two who were injured and lost in the in between. It is not their time. I can do that from my residence."

"Just lay still for a few minutes. Once you feel up to it, I'll take you home."

"Shall I put the kettle on, sir? Nothing like a nice hot cup of tea when you're out of sorts. Everything is still in the kitchen."

"Good idea, Barnes."

A few moments later, Barnes returned carrying a tray with three cups of tea. He set it on an ornately carved side table with bear-claw feet.

"Merci, constable." Amelia sat up and accepted the cup Barnes held towards her. She glanced around the room. "The family has lovely furnishings."

Hodgins stood by the unlit fireplace, nodding. "Yes. Mr. Robinson was a carpenter. Wouldn't mind having a few pieces like these myself."

"Maybe Mrs. Robinson will sell some of the furnishing once she's well. She'll need money to feed the children." Barnes sat in the chair beside the settee. "Violet and I are still furnishing our home."

Hodgins put his cup on the mantle with a clatter. "The will. Has anyone looked into his will? Did he even have one?"

Amelia smiled. "The spirits are calmer. Mr. Robinson is pleased you admire his work." She closed her eyes and leaned back. "The key is in the flowers." Her eyes opened. "Does that mean anything to you?"

Hodgins and Barnes looked at each other and shrugged. "It's too cold for any flowers to still be out, and I don't recall seeing any in the house." Hodgins turned to Amelia. "Are you certain she said flowers?"

"Oui. She's repeating 'flower'. You have the house key. Is there another you seek?"

Barnes snapped his fingers. "The desk. One drawer is locked. What about the killer? Who is he?"

Amelia closed her eyes again., then spoke a moment later. "I hear the name Olive repeated over and over. She was the one to be married, non?"

"Oui. I mean yes." Barnes scooched to the edge of the chair. "This is amazing. According to my mother, Great Aunt Cora could get the spirits to make a noise or move things. Can you do that?"

"It does happen, but rarely. Mostly, it is nothing more than a parlour trick. The spirits here are strong, though. I can try."

"Maybe they can knock if the killer is someone Olive knows?"

"Barnes—" Hodgins turned just as a picture frame toppled over on the long side-table near the desk.

"Sir!"

"Coincidence." Hodgins walked over and righted the picture. He stood at the table, staring at it.

A smile crept across Amelia's face. "The picture, it is of Olive, is it not?"

Hodgins slowly turned to face her. "Yes."

"Am I turning you into a believer yet, Detective?"

"Let's just say I'm less skeptical than I was a few days ago.

"Please arrange for me to come back another day to help the older spirits transition. And Miss Olive. Such a violent death has left her, how you say? Stuck? The father will go when he feels vindicated."

* * *

After taking Amelia and Barnes to their respective homes, Hodgins picked up his family and went for a long ride outside the city. By the time he returned from the livery, Beryl had their supper started. Cordelia took over so the nanny could return to her own family. Sara sat at the table, helping the twins with their meal.

Hodgins stood at the doorway, watching. "Those two look like they're about to fall asleep."

Cordelia turned. "I agree. Sara, I think that's enough. Why don't you help your father get them in bed?"

"Yes, Mama." Sara picked up Holly. Hodgins walked over and took Ivy.

A few minutes later, Hodgins returned to the kitchen.

"They can't be in bed already?"

"No. Sara said she could manage. She's grown up so much since we adopted the twins."

Cordelia took the almost empty plates off the table. "Yes. She's a tremendous help. I'm glad. It's allowed Beryl to have the weekends to herself. This morning I found out she has a new beau. I'm afraid we may lose her next year." She handed Hodgins a knife. "You prepare the carrots and tell me what happened at the house with Amelia before Sara comes back down."

Hodgins scraped and cut while Cordelia washed the potatoes. "Well, it got off to a bit of a shaky start. Amelia fainted shortly after entering. Said the spirits overwhelmed her, but they eventually calmed down. Said one puzzling thing. *The key is in the flowers.* There are no flowers at this time of year."

Cordelia put the potato down and began laughing.

"It's strange, but not that strange." Hodgins frowned, not enjoying being made fun of.

"No. You misunderstand. Look." Cordelia reached up and moved some canisters on the shelf. She removed a small tin with *flour* painted on the side and opened it, tilting it so her husband could see inside.

"You hide money in a flour tin? Oh, that kind of flour. I would never have thought of that. As usual, you are amazing."

"It's something most married women do. We try to be as frugal as possible with the household allowance, so we have extra money for Christmas and birthday gifts. Maybe even a new dress or hat."

"You do realize with my investments you don't need secret money?"

"An old habit from before I knew about our financial situation. When we lived with my parents, I used an empty creme jar on my dressing table."

Cordelia picked up the potato and began cutting it. "I hope you won't be angry, but I must confess another secret. I've taken a little of the money and opened accounts for the children."

"Angry for looking out for our family? Never. May I be so bold as to ask where?"

"The Bank of Toronto on Church Street, where your accounts are. I put a little in every month."

He leaned over and kissed her on the cheek. "Wish I'd thought of that. May I assume you have your own account as well?"

Cordelia blushed.

"Good for you. Would you be upset if I contributed as well, or would you prefer to keep this to yourself?"

"I'd like to keep my own as it is, but money for the children would be nice, just in case something happens to us."

"I'll arrange a small monthly transfer as soon as I can." Hodgins made a mental note to slip an extra dollar in Delia's flour tin now and then as well. Every day at work, he faced the possibility of not returning home and wanted her to have quick access to cash if that day came. Scraps barked, interrupting his thoughts, and trotted across the kitchen to greet Sara.

"Holly and Ivy fell asleep as soon as I tucked them in. Did Miss Amelia help you today, Papa?"

"Yes, I believe she did. She kept saying Olive, so maybe one of her acquaintances is responsible, which is what we originally thought. I still need to confirm George Franklin's alibi. Said he was vising people down in Detroit. I've sent a wire to confirm. Don't really feel like making the trip myself. Should hear back any time."

CHAPTER TWENTY-THREE

Hodgins called Barnes into his office the next day to review their notes and list of suspects. Sergeant Cooper knocked on the door and peeked in.

"Telegram from Detroit."

"Great. Grab that, would you, Barnes?"

Cooper handed the telegram to the constable and returned to the desk. Hodgins waited while Barnes read it.

"Is it good news?"

Barnes re-read the telegram, frowning. "I think so. Seems like Franklin really was in Detroit. Guess that's one less suspect, so I suppose that makes it good news." He slid it across the desk so Hodgins could read it.

"One less is good." He picked up his pencil and crossed Franklin's name off his list. "I think we need to focus on Wright's friends."

Barnes nodded. "Just like the medium said."

Hodgins laughed. "Prefer to trust my instincts and the facts. That was a rather interesting display yesterday, though. Would've been nice to get a name. We'll just have to use our brains."

"Anything new on the gambling?"

"No. Haven't heard from Billy in a few days. I hope nothing happened to him. Don't want him winding up a hospital mate with Riddell. I'll pop in later for an update on his condition. The women, too. I do hope they recover. The boys and baby need their mother."

"So, who does your instinct tell you the murderer is? Thomms? We already know he's dishonest."

"Not sure, but I believe it's one of those five lads."

Barnes picked up the notes and read through the comments Hodgins added from the interviews he had when he went back to the university. "You spoke with Thomms and Lockerby in the auditorium. Since we believe we're looking for someone wearing a disguise, maybe someone in the pantomime did it. They'd know about making costumes and disguises."

"Yes, that make sense. Ask around and find out if any of the other friends are involved in the production or maybe had some sort of disagreement with Sam or Olive. I'll pop over to the hospital, then go back to the Robinsons and look for that key.

After visiting with Riddell, Hodgins inquired as to the condition of Mrs. Robinson and her sister, Miss Shore.

The doctor put down the chart he'd been reading. "They both woke early this morning, one after the other. Strange. It was almost as though someone called them back from death's door."

Hodgins thought of Amelia and smiled. *She said she could help them from home.*

The doctor indicated for Hodgins to follow. "You can speak with them, but you aren't going to like their answers." He opened a door down the hall from the nurse's station. "In here."

Hodgins followed the doctor, who stopped at the first bed.

"This is Miss Shore. Mrs. Robinson is in the next bed. Ladies, this is Detective Hodgins." He turned to Hodgins. "I need to see other patients. Please don't stay for more than a few minutes."

As soon as the door closed, Hodgins moved between the beds.

"Ladies, I won't stay long, as I know you need to recover. Can either of you tell me who's responsible for the attack? He looked from one to the other, hoping one of them saw his face.

Miss Shore shook her head. Hodgins turned to her sister.

"Mrs. Robinson?"

"I remember running downstairs, but not why. Afraid I have little memory of anything after retiring for the evening. My sister can't recall anything either."

Hodgins' shoulders dropped. The only people who could tell him what happened had no memory.

"The doctor told us why we are here. Can you tell me where my children are?"

Hodgins hadn't expected them to know anything about the murders yet. He assumed they needed time to heal first.

"It's all right. I know about Jacob and Olive. The doctor didn't know about the boys and baby." Mrs. Robinson wrung her hands. "Where are they? Does Mother have them?"

Relieved at not having to break the news, Hodgins relaxed.

"I'm surprised the doctor told you. Would have thought the shock would do you more harm. The baby is with your mother and the boys are at the Hogabooms. It was actually their daughter who found Olive when she brought the wedding dress over."

"I insisted he tell me something. Unfortunately, he couldn't tell me much."

"She was hysterical. The doctor had to tell her to quiet her." Miss Shore propped herself up against the pillows, wincing. "Other than a headache, we both feel fine and would like to go home."

Hodgins pictures the blood in Olive's room. *Need to get someone to clean the house first.*

"I'm sure the doctor wants to make certain you're both well enough before releasing you. You've been unconscious for days. Get some rest now. I'll make sure someone sends word to your mother and the boys. If you remember anything, please send for me."

As Hodgins walked back to the station, he had mixed feelings about the women waking up: happy they survived, but disappointed they had no memory of the events. Someone would have to clean up Olive's room and the workshop before the ladies returned home and gathered the children.

* * *

Hodgins got the house key from Barnes, then walked over to the Robinson's. He noticed most people crossed the street to avoid passing too close to the now deserted home. The newspapers were calling it the murder house. He didn't bother re-locking the door after he entered.

As he passed the sitting room, he glanced in. The picture of Olive fell over again. Hodgins hesitated before going in, stopping a few feet in front of the table.

"I get it," he mumbled. "We're looking into Mr. Wright's friends. I've come to look for the key in the flour tin."

A chilly breeze swirled around him, then vanished as quickly as it came. Hodgins took the last two steps and righted the picture.

He shook his head. "Must be crazy, talking to ghosts."

It didn't take long to find the flour tin. He dumped the contents into a bowl and sifted through it with a fork. After a few minutes of poking through the flour, the fork hit something solid. A tiny key hung on one tine. Hodgins smiled. "Thanks, Delia." He paused. "And you too, Olive."

He got most of the flour back into the tin, wiping the spillage into the sink and flushing it with a few strokes of the pump.

When he returned to the front room, he glanced at the picture and held up the key. The breeze returned, rustling the paper on the desk.

"I know. I know." Hodgins continued to mumble as he tried the key. It fit the locked drawer, clicking when turned. A single envelope sat on the bottom.

"That's it? What is so important about that one letter that Mr. Robinson felt the need to lock it up?"

Hodgins picked it up and turned it over. "Hmm. No return address." He opened the envelope and removed the letter. The handwriting was scratchy and difficult to read.

Again, no return address at the top of the letter, but it had a date—two days before the murder. Instead of a signature, he'd signed it *The Better Man.*

"Delia was right. It's all about love."

CHAPTER TWENTY-FOUR

Hodgins sat in his office, still trying to figure out who wrote the letter when Barnes returned to the station.

The constable hurried over. "None of the other lads are in the pantomime, only Thomms and Lockerby. Simmons took part last year, but his grades have slipped so far down they wouldn't allow him to join this year."

Hodgins raised an eyebrow. "They only returned to school two months ago. Hardly seems long enough to have grades that low."

Barnes pulled the chair over close to Hodgins' desk. "I thought it rather peculiar myself. Seems like he either hasn't handed in assignments, or they were late and poorly written."

"Did he offer any explanation?"

"No, sir. Couldn't find him. Seems he's decided to play hooky for the last few days."

"Interesting." Hodgins slid the letter across his desk. "What do you make of this?"

Barnes picked it up and tilted his head. "Not the easiest to read." He turned the paper a few times, trying to get a better angle. "I can provide for her better." Barnes looked at Hodgins. "Could he be referring to Olive?"

"Yes, I believe so. Doesn't really narrow it down, though. All the lads have money. Rather, their fathers do. No other way to afford university. Unfortunately, the only one we know who was excessively interested in Olive doesn't have money and was in Detroit."

"I guess one of the lads hasn't been completely truthful with us."

"I think we need to have another chat with Wright's friends, and Robinson's neighbours as well. Find out if another young man has been around more than usual. You talk to the people on Wilton and Pembroke. I'll take George Street."

Hodgins started with Olive's friend who lived across the road from the Robinson's. Charlotte Carter mentioned they were best friends. If someone other than Sam Wright was showing interest, she'd know. Her mother answered the door.

"You're that detective, aren't you?"

"Yes, ma'am. Is your daughter home? I'd like to speak with her."

"Charlotte is still quite upset. Can it wait?"

"No, afraid not. She may have information that can help catch the person responsible."

Mrs. Carter hesitated. "Well, I don't know."

"I just have one question. Won't take long."

"Come in, then. She's in the front parlour. This way."

Mrs. Carter stopped at the first door on the left. "Charlotte, the detective has a question for you."

Charlotte looked up from her book, her eyes red and puffy. "Have you found the person who killed my friend?"

Hodgins stepped into the room. "No, but you may be able to help. Has anyone other than her fiancé been around? Someone interested in Olive?"

Charlotte dropper to book onto her lap. "No, of course not. Olive loved Sam. She'd never entertain another gentleman."

Mrs. Carter sat beside her, putting her arm around Charlotte's shoulders. "Please, detective. Charlotte is much too distraught."

"I'm sorry, but I need to know. I'm not suggesting she was unfaithful, but maybe someone was perusing her?"

Charlotte sniffled. "Well…"

"Please. If you know anything, I need you to tell me. For Olive and her family."

"She told me one of Sam's friends had been rather forward. Olive never said his name, but I saw someone over there a few times. Mr. Robinson had words with him at the front door a few days before the murders. I couldn't hear, but I could tell he was angry. The young man tried to push his way in, but Mr. Robinson shoved him back and closed the door."

"What did the young man look like?"

"Taller than Mr. Robinson. When he turned to leave, I noticed a mustache. And I could tell his overcoat was dark brown, and quite expensive looking."

Hodgins wrote down everything she said. "Thank you. You've helped more than you can imagine. Now I just need to prove it."

Charlotte smiled. "Really?"

"Really. Again, thank you. I can see myself out."

Hodgins checked with the other neighbours. Most recalled the tall, mustached young man, but couldn't say when he was around. Hodgins caught up with Barnes down the street and they walked back to the station house.

"Afraid I had no luck, sir. No one recalls anything out of the ordinary."

"I had a hunch and began with Olive's best friend. She admitted Olive told her someone had been trying to court her. Didn't have a name, but she witnessed an altercation between one of Sam's friends and Mr. Robinson. The description matches Matthew Simmons."

"Simmons? Do you think he did it? Didn't seem the type."

"They rarely do. We need to find out what the argument was about. Could be anything. It's a place to start, though. I saw in the paper Sam Wright's funeral is tomorrow afternoon. His friends should be there. With any luck, Simmons will surface. I'll try to speak with him when the service is over. I want you to come too, just in case there's trouble."

CHAPTER TWENTY-FIVE

Hodgins directed the driver to stop the horse on Wellesley Street, away from the buggies parked around St. James Cemetery. He didn't ask the driver to wait, as he didn't know how long they'd be.

"This is the cemetery where that young girl was buried last year. Noisy, isn't it?" Barnes looked around, trying to catch a glimpse of the Don River.

"Yes. I haven't been here since. Strange coincidence. Her name was Olive, and she lived close to the Robinson family, but this Olive won't be buried here." Hodgins checked the time on his pocket watch. "Should start soon. People are heading into the chapel. May as well go to the cemetery. Stay out of the way, though."

A light snow fell overnight, coating the ground and headstones with a thin white blanket. Hodgins pointed. "See that mound of dirt? Looks like his grave over there. We can stand in the trees a few yards away. The service inside the chapel will probably take at least thirty minutes. Come with me."

Hodgins led Barnes to the back of the cemetery. The roar of the river made it almost impossible to talk.

"Sir! It's unbelievable." Barnes peered through the trees at the river below. Because the snow that had been falling, then melting during the heat wave, the banks had risen.

Hodgins leaned close and spoke in Barnes' ear. "You need to see it in early spring. Twice as fast."

They stood watching for about twenty minutes, then Hodgins tapped Barnes' arm and nodded his head, indicating they needed to return to the grave. The doors of the tiny chapel finally opened, and the mourners filed out.

"Looks like most of Wright's classmates are here." Barnes raised his collar as an icy wind whipped around the trees.

"And if I'm not mistaken, Principal McCaul and George Franklin as well." Hodgins pointed. "There's Simmons. Keep an eye on him. We need to catch him before he leaves."

Once they lowered the coffin and the last few words were spoken, the crowds around the grave thinned. Wright's five school chums remained behind. The detective and constable approached. Thomms noticed them first and sneered.

"You here to harass me again, detective?"

"Just doing my job. Sorry if you feel harassed. I'm actually here to speak with Mr. Simmons." Hodgins turned. "You're a hard man to find these days. I've come across some information that I need you to clarify."

"I've just buried one of my dearest friends. It will have to wait."

"Afraid I can't wait. Speak to me now or down at the station."

"You'll have to wait until tomorrow."

Hodgins turned to see who spoke.

"I'm Matthew's father. He's coming home with me."

"I understand, but it is urgent. I'm trying to find out who murdered his friend. Friends, actually. We believe the same person killed Miss Robinson and her father. Three people in total. I must insist."

Mr. Simmons mulled over what Hodgins said. "I agree. Urgency is required, just not today. I don't know if you're aware, but I'm a lawyer. If you aren't arresting him right now, I'll bring my son in tomorrow morning. Nine o'clock agreeable?"

Hodgins nodded.

"Good. Matthew, boys, come along. Everyone is waiting."

"Do you believe he'll bring his son in?"

Hodgins sighed. "Seems like I have no choice but to wait and find out. I just hope he allows his son to answer my questions."

* * *

By nine-thirty the next morning, Hodgins was furious. "Where the blazes are they? I'm not waiting any longer." Hodgins grabbed his overcoat off the coat tree. The tree toppled, narrowly missing the hot stove.

Barnes rushed over to pick it up. "You nearly knocked over the kettle, sir." He grinned at the detective.

Hodgins took a deep breath, then chuckled. "Can't have the fellows going without their tea, now can we? Guess I need to calm myself before confronting the lawyer."

"Sir, look. Mr. Simmons is here, but he's alone."

The lawyer stood just inside the door, looking around. When he spotted Hodgins, he approached. "I can't find Matthew. We haven't seen him since supper."

CHAPTER TWENTY-SIX

Hodgins escorted Simmons into his office, instructing Barnes to fetch tea. He gestured for Simmons to take the chair in front of his desk. "Do you think your son went for a walk and forgot the time?" He wanted to give the lad the benefit of the doubt.

Simmons sighed. "No. My wife checked his room. His travel bag is missing, as are his toiletries and some clothing. He's run off." Simmons slammed his fist on Hodgins' desk. "How could he have done such a thing? Why would he commit murder?" His voice quivered. "And with three little boys in the house."

Barnes came in and sat two cups of tea on the desk. Hodgins waved him out, then waited while Simmons composed himself.

"We don't know for certain he killed anyone. Maybe he saw something or someone and was frightened off."

Simmons picked up the teacup but didn't drink. "My wife begged me not to come. Almost didn't. If he's guilty, he'll hang. As a lawyer, if he were a client, I'd tell his parents to alert the police so they could make an arrest. But it's my son. I've done my duty informing you he's gone, but I won't help you find him."

He put the cup down and left.

Hodgins waved Barnes in. "Young Simmons has packed a bag and scarpered. His father won't provide any additional information. I understand completely. If one of my girls was in this type of trouble, I'd not be forthcoming with information that would lead to their death."

Barnes dropped into the chair vacated by Simmons. "Do we know how much of a head start he got?"

"Afraid not. Mr. Simmons said they haven't seen him since supper. Unless he's withholding the exact time his son left, I'm guessing it was during the night. His parents would likely have heard the door otherwise."

"Can't be easy, believing your son did something so horrible. Fastest way out would be the train. I'll check the schedules to see what trains may have left overnight, as well as early evening, just in case."

"No, I'll do that. I want to you get a picture of him and have copies made. If the family won't oblige, check with the university."

Barnes stood, but didn't leave. "Um, I think I'll go straight to the school."

Hodgins nodded. "Probably best. And see if you can get a sample of his writing. Must have an essay or something in his file."

By the time Barnes returned, Hodgins had a short list of possible escape trains. "Make sure some of the lads get copies, just in case the boy hasn't left town. I'll take one down to Union Station."

Barnes looked at the list Hodgins made.

- *Detroit: Grand Trunk: 7:30 a.m. mail train, 7:15 p.m. third class, 1:35 a.m. second class*

- *Owen Sound: 8:00 a.m. mail train, 5:00 p.m. accommodation train*

- *Coboconk: 7:45 a.m. mail train, 4:00 p.m. local*

"If it was me, I'd head to Detroit. Get out of the country."

Hodgins agreed. "Probably figures crossing the border would be his safest route. Why don't you check the ships? Someone may have been desperate enough to take on a soft kid like Simmons."

Barnes headed to a small room at the back of the station. It had recently been transformed into a dark room and Barnes had been eager to learn everything he could so they wouldn't have to rely on the one officer who had been acting as their new official photographer. Thirty minutes later, he emerged with six copies. He handed one to

Hodgins, gave four to the constables, and kept the last for himself.

"Sorry they aren't very sharp, sir. I took a picture of the photograph so it's not the best, but you can still make out his features quite nicely."

"Not to worry. They're more than adequate. I went out and waved over a cab while waiting. Horse doesn't look like the fastest, but it'll get us where we're going. Let's head out before the nag falls asleep."

They made good time, despite getting stuck behind a wagon loaded with barrels. Hodgins got off at Union Station and paid the driver enough to cover the additional trip to drop Barnes at the docks.

A train was pulling out when Hodgins arrived, so there weren't many people milling around. He went to the ticket window, picture in hand. Most of the ticket agents knew Hodgins.

"Morning, Harold. Don't suppose you've seen this lad today?" Hodgins slid the picture through the opening in the glass.

Harold picked up the photograph. "Doesn't look familiar. Guess if you're looking for him, he's not as innocent as he looks."

"Person of interest at the moment. Let's just say I'm highly motivated to find him. Anyone around from the overnight shift who may have seen him?"

"I'll ask around. Give me a minute. I think Charlie's napping in the back. Doesn't like going home after the graveyard shift. Thinks he's gonna get attacked or something." Harold chuckled. "I'll see if one of the other fellas remembers him."

Hodgins watched as heads shook *no*. Harold opened a door and disappeared into another room. Less than a minute later, Harold rushed to the ticket window.

"Charlie thinks he saw him. Come 'round and I'll let you in. He's not pleased I woke him."

Hodgins walked to the end of the counter where Harold held the hinged section open. The detective headed straight for the room where Charlie napped. The off-duty ticket agent was already back asleep and snoring. Hodgins grabbed his shoulder and shook him.

"Charlie. Wake up."

An arm shot out, catching Hodgins across his chest.

"Blast it all, Charlie. Wake up before I arrest you for striking an officer."

Charlie's eyes popped open. "Wha? Arrest me? Fer what?" He blinked a few times, focusing on Hodgins. "Detective? That you?"

"Sit up, Charlie. I need some information, then I'll take you home."

Charlie swung his legs over the side of the cot and ran his fingers through the remaining tufts of white hair. He perked up when Harold held out a cup of steaming tea.

"Don't suppose you put a bit of Irish in it? No, guess not." He took a sip. "What is it you're wanting?" His voice had a slight Irish lilt.

Hodgins held out the picture. "Harold said you saw this lad. Do you remember what train he took?"

"Give me a minute to clear the cobwebs." Charles gulped down the tea and handed the cup to Harold. "Ah, that's better. Let me think." He took the picture and stared at it for several minutes, mumbling.

"Ah, got it. Took the one-thirty-five in the wee hours this morn. Headed to Detroit, it was. Barely made it. He just wanted a ticket to the next train out, and she was just ready to pull away."

"You're certain?"

"Sure as my name is Charles Seamus O'Casey."

"Right. Promised you a ride. Come on."

"That's a fine offer. May you live to be one hundred years, with one extra year to repent."

Hodgins rolled his eyes. "Not certain if that's a blessing or a curse, but I'll take it. Have to stop at the docks to find my constable first."

***

When he finally arrived back at Station House Four, Hodgins checked the train schedule for Detroit. "Barnes, send a telegram to Chief Constable McCarthy in Stratford. See if he can check the train for Simmons. Train's due in there around eleven-thirty."

Barnes glanced at the time. "That's cutting it rather close. It's already gone eleven."

"So, why are you just standing there? Hurry."

A reply came back just before noon. Barnes ran into Hodgins' office, waving a telegram. "Sir, they got him. Want to know what to do with him."

"Ask if they can bring him back. We can cover the train and one night's accommodation. If no one's willing, then I guess I'll have to travel down."

* * *

Billy waited in the end stall at Mitchell's livery. It had been over a half hour since he'd sent word for the detective to meet him. He peeked over the stall wall when voices echoed through the building. *'Bout bloody time.*

The detective spent a few minutes exchanging pleasantries with the liveryman, leaving Billy waiting even longer.

"I thunk you weren't never gonna git here."

"I have other business to take care of. Can't just drop everything. Next time you might consider asking your runner to wait for a reply. The sergeant has a soft spot for the little ones. Whoever you send will likely end up with nothing more than a full belly and maybe a penny or two. What news do you have?"

Billy sat on a hay bale and leaned against the wall. "Been sent to two different houses with gambling. That fella what got threw outta the game a few weeks back? Thomms? He showed up and never made it more'n a couple steps inside afore they tossed 'im out." Billy grinned. "Heard the splash when he landed in a puddle of melted snow. Another lad was with 'im, and they let him stay when he pulled out a pouch of silver. Heard someone, Thomms, I think, call him Geoff."

Hodgins flipped through his notebook. "Geoffrey Lockerby. They let him stay?"

"Yep. Don't think they knowed him. Must have been his first time. Didn't do too bad at first, then started losing. Knew enough to stop before he lost it all."

"So, he probably doesn't have any gambling debts to speak of. Word would have got around." Hodgins jotted a few notes in his book. "Ever hear the name Moynehan? Officer with a questionable reputation."

Billy shook his head. "Nah. If a bent copper is involved, he ain't been 'round to the gambling houses. Least ways not when I been there."

Hodgins reached into his pocket and handed several coins to Billy. "Thank you for helping out. You can quit now. I worry about you being involved with that rough lot."

Billy waved away the money. "Just got paid. Might stay a little while longer. They may be rough, but they pay pretty good. Just staying with Stretch temporary like."

"Don't do anything foolish."

Billy started to leave, then stopped and turned. "I was thinkin', it's not safe to leave so much money in my space. Word's bound to get 'round I'm flush. Maybe after a few more paydays I could open a bank account? If you wouldn't mind coming with me? Bankers don't look at the likes of me. Won't even let me much past the front door before shooing me out."

"Glad to. Once you have enough, maybe you can get some new clothes and get a proper job."

Billy's jaws dropped. "Work fer someone else, regular like? No way. I like me independence."

Hodgins laughed. "Won't ask you to do anything you don't want to. You know how to reach me. And if one of those gambling houses gets raided while you're there, make sure an officer tells me. I'll find a way to get you out without raising suspicion."

"Ain't no one ever caught me." Billy was off and out the side door before Hodgins could say another word.

* * *

"Sir." Barnes ran into Hodgins' office, painting.

"Sit down and catch your breath. Looks like you just ran a race."

"It's Riddell." Barnes gulped in more air.

Hodgins straightened in his chair. "Don't tell me he didn't make it?"

"No, no. He's going home tomorrow. I just saw him and ran all the way back from the hospital."

The detective relaxed. "That's a relief. What about his eye?"

"The bandage is off. He says his sight is still blurry, but the doctor said it might be a while before they know for certain if he'll see properly. He's trying to get used to crutches. His foot'll be bound for some time. They won't know if that healed properly until they take all the wrappings off. I believe Tom said not for another month. He's not supposed to walk unless necessary. He's anxious to come back to work, even if he can't do regular duties."

"I'll speak with the inspector, just in case. May as well prepare for the worst and hope for the best."

Hodgins tapped his notebook. "Seems like we have another gambler among our groups of university friends. That Lockerby lad went to one of the gambling houses with Thomms. Apparently, Thomms got tossed, but they let Lockerby stay. I guess that one has a little more sense than his friend. I'll have another chat with him."

CHAPTER TWENTY-SEVEN

Late afternoon, Delia came into the station to speak with her husband. "I just spent a lovely afternoon at the museum with Amelia. She's ready to move along the spirits at the Robinson home. Can you pick her up at 11:30 tonight?"

"I think I can manage that. I'd like to see exactly what she does. Tea?"

Before she could answer, Barnes came in with two steaming cups. "It's a might chilly out there. Thought you could use a warm-up."

Cordelia stayed and chatted for a little while, then hurried home to start the evening meal.

At the end of the day, Hodgins hired a small brougham, and at 11:15 p.m. he headed out to pick up Amelia and take her to the Robinson's. She wrapped herself in the blanket that sat beside the detective after placing her satchel on the floor, then settled back. Hodgins flicked the reins and the large black mare lifted its left hind leg to begin his walk along the empty city street.

Hodgins stifled a laugh when the sudden movement caused Amelia to jerk sideways. "Why did you insist on a late night hour for this? When you were at the house before, you said spirits didn't care about time."

"This is different. Before, I just needed to speak with them. Tonight, I need to encourage them to move to the beyond. The veil is thinnest at Samhain, but that has passed. Midnight is the next best time."

Hodgins sighed. "Of course it is." Neither spoke the rest of the way. He tied the horse to the maple, helped Amelia down, and led the way into the house.

The psychic went into the sitting room and sat the satchel on the end table before removing items. She handed Hodgins a box of wooden matches, then placed white candles around the room. The detective followed, lighting them as instructed.

Once she was satisfied with the placement and number of candles, she removed a bundle of something from her bag.

Hodgins raised an eyebrow. "A bouquet of weeds?"

"Non. Not weeds. This is dried white sage. It will help clear the room."

"Of course it will." *Balderdash. Ghosts. Spirits. Hooey.*

Amelia used a candle to light the bundle. Once the flame took hold, she gently blew it out, leaving the sage smoking.

Hodgins took a whiff. "Smells nice."

"I must cleanse every room. Murder leaves negative energy and the sage will help remove it." She walked the perimeter of the sitting room, softly speaking in French. Once the main floor was done, she moved to the foot of the stairs and stopped.

"Detective, please go to my bag. You will find a single white rose. Bring it along."

When he returned, Amelia headed up the stairs, fanning the smoke and whispering in French again. When she got to the doorway of Olive's room, Hodgins stopped her.

"That room hasn't been cleaned up yet. I don't think you want to go in there."

The psychic waved a hand, dismissing him. "The rose, s'il vous plait."

She walked in, going directly to the bed, placed the rose on the pillow, then began speaking, periodically pausing, as though listening to a reply. Loose strands of hair blew across her face.

Hodgins cocked his head. *Where is that breeze coming from? All the doors and windows are closed.* A chill ran down his back.

When finished, she circled the bedroom once again, fanning the smoke.

The candle Hodgins held flickered several times, almost extinguishing itself. *Odd. I felt no breeze.*

"Miss Olive has crossed over, as have the older spirits. Only her father has remained. As I said before, he will go when the killer is caught." She turned to leave, but stopped. Amelia nodded and smiled.

"Her grandfather reached out. He will watch over the family when they return. I expect the father will, as well. We can go now."

"Good. It's freezing in here." *And creepy.* "Have to remember to make sure fires are lit before Mrs. Robinson returns with the children. Thank you for your assistance."

They extinguished all the candles and packed them away, then Amelia went into the kitchen and returned with a plate.

"What's that for?"

She put the plate on the end table and placed the smoldering sage on it. "The sage will burn down, to ensure the home is cleansed. The plate is to prevent a fire."

"You know," Hodgins hesitated. "It somehow feels different in here. Dangdest thing."

Amelia smiled. "Oui, the house is happy now."

"A happy house. Sure, why not?" Hodgins carried her bag out and helped her into the brougham.

After taking her home, Hodgins returned the buggy to the livery. Caleb had hidden a key so the detective could put the horse in the stall. He wiped down the mare, locked up, leaving the key in the hiding place as directed, then wrapped a blanket around his shoulders and walked home. He'd return it to Caleb in the morning.

CHAPTER TWENTY-EIGHT

The next day, winter tried to take hold again. Hodgins took a cab down to Union Station in the midst of a sudden squall to pick up Simmons and the officer escorting him. He paid the driver extra to wait and went inside to stand by the wood stove. The driver threw a blanket over the horse to protect it from the snow.

"Morning, Harold. Charlie still here?"

The ticket agent shook his head and came out from behind the ticket desk and joined Hodgins. "Just missed him. Need more information from him?"

"No." Hodgins held his hands over the stove to warm them. "Just wanted to thank him. We got the lad when the train pulled into Stratford. Just waiting for the train back. An officer is bringing our escapee home."

"Far as I know, it's on schedule. Should be here in five minutes. Is he responsible for the death of those people in the newspaper?"

"It's looking like it. I have no clear motive, though. Not for him or anyone else."

Both men turned when someone rapped repeatedly on the counter. An elderly gentleman scowled at the ticket agent.

Harold chuckled. "Looks like I have an impatient customer. Best of luck with the lad." He went back behind the ticket counter and Hodgins headed out to the platform to watch for the train.

A few minutes later, a whistle blew and brakes screeched. Hodgins scanned the passengers as they disembarked, looking for a uniformed officer. Instead, he saw a well-dressed man escorting a handcuffed Simmons. He walked over to them.

"Welcome home, Mr. Simmons. Too bad you didn't make it to Detroit." he turned to the gentleman. "I'm Detective Hodgins. I expected to see a constable with him."

The gentleman extended a hand. "Chief Constable McCarthy. Haven't had a chance to visit the city for a long time, so I thought I'd bring him myself. Staying an extra day or two. Was hoping you could recommend a suitable hotel."

"Certainly." Hodgins relieved the cuffed Simmons of the satchel he held in front of him. "Got a cabriolet waiting. This way. Let's see. The Bay Horse on Yonge Street. It's close to everything and is clean and affordable. I'll have the driver go up Yonge and point it out. If you want to check in now, we can wait."

Once they arrived at the station, Hodgins gave McCarthy a tour while Barnes took Simmons into the interrogation room.

McCarthy seemed impressed at the size of the station. "We have nothing quite this large in Stratford. If you don't mind me asking, what did the lad do?"

"Surprised it hasn't reached your newspapers. Have you heard about the family attacked here a couple of weeks ago? And the university student?"

"Yes. Both the *Beacon* and *Harold* had stories. Ghastly." McCarthy stopped. "You mean to tell me young Simmons did that? Unbelievable."

Hodgins agreed. "We don't know for certain, but hopping on a train doesn't make him look innocent. Don't suppose he said anything on the way here?"

"Not a word. Just stared out the window. Why would he do such a thing?"

"That's what we can't figure out. Care to sit in on the interrogation?"

"Yes, thank you."

They made a stop at Hodgins' office so he could retrieve the file with all his notes. When they went into the interrogation room, Simmons sat slumped in one of the chairs, head hanging down.

"He hasn't said a word, sir. I asked if he wanted his father, and he just shrugged."

"Very well, Barnes. You may as well fetch him. He'll most likely need a lawyer, as well as his father. I hope for now, the elder Simmons is feeling more fatherly."

Hodgins sat opposite the lad. McCarthy stood by the door.

"Mr. Simmons. Matthew. I've sent for your father. Do you have anything to say before he arrives?"

Loud voices carried down the corridor from the front of the station, then the door flew open, almost hitting McCarthy.

"Out of my way." Mr. Simmons senior shoved Barnes aside and stormed in.

"Sir, he barged in before I could stop him."

"Word got back to me that you found my boy and were bringing him home today. I insist on speaking with him. Alone."

Hodgins rose. "You have five minutes." He picked up the file and nodded to McCarthy.

Hodgins closed the door behind him and waited in the hall with Barnes and the chief constable. "His father is a lawyer."

McCarthy nodded.

The hollering started as soon as the latch clicked shut. The only voice they heard was the father.

"Guess he's here as a father." Barnes grinned as the yelling continued.

When the five minutes were up, Hodgins opened the door.

"Time's up. I need to question your son."

"Good luck with that. He's not talking."

Hodgins looked at McCarthy and mumbled. "He never had a chance."

McCarthy stifled a laugh. Mr. Simmons scowled and began pacing. Hodgins pulled a chair beside Matthew and opened the file.

"I believe you wrote this?" He slid the note from Mr. Robinson's desk in front of the lad. "You are *The Better Choice*?"

Matthew glanced at it, but remained silent.

Hodgins placed another page over the top of the letter.

"This is one of your school essays. The handwriting matches. What did you mean, *better choice*?"

Mr. Simmons senior stopped pacing long enough to grab both papers. He read the letter, then compared it to the essay.

"Did you write this letter?"

Matthew stared at the tabletop.

"Answer me, boy." Simmons senior shook his son's shoulder.

Matthew blinked a few times. "What?"

His father waved the letter in front of his son's face. "Did you write this?"

"Yes."

Hodgins watched as Mr. Simmons' anger melted away. He got up and gestured for him to sit and speak with his son, then moved to a chair on the opposite side of the table.

"I don't understand. Sam was your friend. He was going to marry Olive, and you were to stand with him. Why would you kill Olive and her father days before the wedding? And Sam? You did that as well?"

"I had to. Don't you see that?"

Hodgins set his notebook on the table and turned to a fresh page. "Matthew. Tell me what happened two weeks ago when you went to the Robinsons."

"I went over early so I could talk to Mr. Robinson before school. He was already up. I heard him in the workshop so I went around back. I begged him to tell Olive she should marry me. Our family is wealthier than Sam's. I could provide for her so much better. He refused."

Hodgins wrote quickly, trying to keep up with the confession. He looked up when Matthew stopped, then quickly added the rest of the notes.

Mr. Simmons put his arm around Matthew as the young man began weeping.

"Can you do this later? He's quite upset," Simmons senior asked.

"I'm sorry, but I need to know. It won't be any easier on him later. Might make him feel better once he gets it off his chest."

"It's all right, Father." Matthew pulled out a handkerchief, blew his nose, then continued.

"Mr. Robinson told me to leave. I became furious and picked up a piece of wood from his workbench and hit him. I was so angry I just kept hitting him over and over. When I realized what I'd done, I covered him with some old sacks."

McCarthy reached for Hodgins' file. "May I?"

"Go ahead. So far, his account matches what we found at the house." Hodgins turned to Matthew. "What about Olive?"

"I went in the back door and upstairs. Olive was still sleeping. I woke her and asked her to run away with me. She screamed, but I put my hand over her mouth before she woke the household. When she realized it was me, she calmed down. She thought it was a prank and laughed at me. I had to shut her up. I'd grabbed a knife when I went through the kitchen and stabbed Olive before I realized what I was doing.

"Her mother must have heard the scream and woke. When I turned, she was standing at the bedroom door. She ran downstairs, so I tossed the knife into the room across the hall, then chased her. Olive's aunt woke and followed. I grabbed the poker and hit them both. Mrs. Robinson went down right away. Olive's aunt ran out of the room. I chased her into a small room and hit her several times. Wiped the poker off on Mrs. Robinson's nightgown, then ran."

"At least the rest of the children weren't harmed. Why kill Sam later?"

"He was so upset, I just wanted him to be at peace. Now Sam and Olive can be united and wed in heaven."

The detective put down his pencil. "But why the disguise?"

Geoffrey looked puzzled. "Disguise?"

"Yes. The red wig and mutton chops."

"I wore no disguise."

CHAPTER TWENTY-NINE

Once Matthew was formally charged, arrested, and locked up, Barnes and McCarthy joined Hodgins in his office.

"Sir, I'm confused about the red-haired man."

"As am I," McCarthy said. "According to your notes, several people saw him around both murders."

"Coincidence, possibly? It's not against the law to have red hair. We have no evidence that the red-haired man committed a crime. The student that saw him arguing with Sam may have simply been having a disagreement. Maybe the neighbour really did see a peeper in the neighbourhood. As for the stolen wig, it may merely have been misplaced."

"Peculiar, though." Barnes tapped his fingers on Hodgins' desk. "What about the pile of old clothes and boots?"

"They don't appear to be connected to the murders. Hopefully, when Mrs. Robinson regains her memory, we'll find out. Anyway, Henry. I promised Stonehouse we'd have him to dinner once this was over to meet Cordelia's friend,

Amelia. Circumstances have caused them to meet already, but a promise is a promise. Why don't you and Violet join us? McCarthy, since you're staying a few days, why don't to come along, too? Afraid the only lady I can match you up with to balance the table will be my ten-year-old, Sara. I can promise she'll be full of questions. Tomorrow or the next night work for you both? I need to check with Delia, of course."

McCarthy smiled. "Be my honour."

"I know Violet would love to see the twins again. Count on us."

* * *

Henry and Violet Barnes came early so Violet could play with the twins. When McCarthy arrived, he sat with the men in the front room. Doctor Stonehouse and Amelia arrived shortly after. Amelia joined Delia in the kitchen, leaving the men to their whisky.

"Violet certainly has taken to the twins, Henry. I'd say she's ready to start a family."

"She wants a house-full. Not sure I want that many, but we'll have to see what happens. They'll all be welcome."

Hodgins turned his attention to the doctor. "Delia tells me you've been spending a lot of time with Amelia over the past several days. Too soon to ask about wedding plans, I suppose?"

Stonehouse almost choked on his whisky. "I only met the woman a week ago. We do get along quite well, though. Not to change the subject, but I heard your constable is going home. Riddell, is it?" He turned to McCarthy. "Took quite a beating."

"Glad to hear he's okay. I lost one of mine last year in a shooting."

Sara popped into the front room, wearing her best dress. "Mommy says dinner is ready."

McCarthy stood and walked over to Sara. "Since I'm your dinner companion, would you care to accompany me to the table?" He held his arm out for her.

Sara giggled and took the offered arm. "This way."

* * *

Once dessert was over and the conversation died down, the guests headed to the front door. Just as Amelia entered the front hall, she stumbled and reached for the door frame. Stonehouse took her arm and lead her to the nearest chair.

"Are you all right? You've gone pale."

"I am fine, merci. I had a vision. A baby boy, kidnapped. The vision is gone now."

"Gracious." Cordelia poured a small glass of brandy and handed it to Amelia. "Are you certain? Who's baby?"

Amelia shook her head. "I do not know, but I saw both you and your husband's faces flash through my mind."

Cordelia looked at her husband. "We know no one who has a baby. Maybe you're just tired from all the excitement with the murders."

"My visions are never wrong. If I see any anything else, I will let you know. Thank you for a pleasant evening." Amelia stood, still a little dizzy.

Stonehouse slipped his arm around her tiny waist. "Lean on me. You need rest. I'll see you home safely."

As soon as everyone left, Cordelia turned to her husband. "Are you still a skeptic? Do you believe someone's baby will be taken?"

"Nonsense. I believe she has some sort of gift, but seeing future events? No. I do, however, predict the doctor will pay many more social calls on her, though."

Cordelia smiled. "Yes, I quite agree. It's been a tiring day and long past time to retire. The dishes can wait until morning."

She slipped her hand in his and headed upstairs.

Reviews are Golden

I would love to hear from you! Please consider leaving a review on your favourite social media platform, Amazon, or Goodreads.

Reviews mean the world to authors. Not only do we enjoy reading how you felt about the book, but they help other readers get a feel for a book in advance, and aid authors in marketing.

If you wish to hear about the progress of any of my books, please join my newsletter at:
https://landing.mailerlite.com/webforms/landing/u0q5f2

Thank you for coming on this adventure with me.

ABOUT THE AUTHOR

Nanci M. Pattenden is a genealogist and an emerging fiction writer, currently working on a collection of detective stories set in Victorian Toronto and an Urban Fantasy trilogy. She also co-authors a funny paranormal series, D.E.M.ON. Tales.

She has completed the Creative Writing program at both the University of Calgary and the University of Toronto.

Nanci currently resides in Newmarket with her fluffy cat Snowball.

nanci@nancipattenden.com
www.murderdoespayink.ca
www.nancipattenden.com
@npattenden